City of Strangers

By
Diane Rivers

Bella
BOOKS

2010

Bella Books, Inc.
P.O. Box 10543
Tallahassee, FL 32302

Printed in the United States of America on acid-free paper
First edition

Editor: Medora MacDougall
Cover Illustration: Cedar Kindy
Cover Designer: Judy Fellows

ISBN 10: 1-59493-183-6
ISBN 13:978-1-59493-183-3

This book is dedicated to all the women who over the years have listened to my stories and given me support and encouragement.

About the Author

Diana Rivers lives in the hills of Arkansas on women's land, in a community of women who sustain her life and nurture her existence. Her house, that she designed herself, was all built by women's hands, including her own. She has a girlfriend who lives right across the yard, a cat and dog and many characters that keep her company, a wonderful view, a little vegetable garden that she tries to remember to weed and water, and now, in spite of much resistance, a computer which is often her friend but sometimes her enemy. She has written many poems, several short stories that were published in feminist magazines, and performance pieces for Goddess Productions, a readers' theater troupe, as well as six books in the Hadra series. This book is her first venture into a new and different world.

This is the day, I thought as I stood looking out the window of my room in the Palace, high above the city of Hernorium, this city that held me captive. *Before this day is over I will be either dead or gone.*

This was the first day I was to be allowed out in the city streets and I was ready. I had no fear, only a hard determination at my core that all of Peltron's threats of violence and all of Torvin's loving kindness could not alter. I felt a momentary pang for the sorrow I would cause Torvin who, all things considered, was a kind, good man in a hard place—but it was not enough to change my course and spare him grief. One way or the other I would be free before day's end, of that much I was sure.

Mist rose from the streets, shifting about, obscuring, then revealing different parts of the city in patches of shade and brilliance. A thicker mist rose from the lake where the boat races were to be held later that day, a twirling dance of white and gray moving over the surface of the water. Beyond the lake and almost hidden by the mist lay a vast plain, the food basket for the city, with its patchwork of farms and fields and roads. And beyond that rose the dark woods that were my path home, though having been brought to this city bound and blindfolded I was not yet sure of my way back.

Peltron and his men had captured me when I was walking alone in the woods, a fair distance from home and many days' ride away from this strange city. I had supposedly gone to hunt for mushrooms, but in truth I was indulging my foul mood, going along scuffing up leaves and kicking rocks in my ill temper at my lover, Adana. My mushroom bag was empty, and I was paying scant attention to my surroundings, unusual for me.

I had been following a narrow, twisting and not very clear path through the trees, not at all sure I knew where I was, when the way ended abruptly at an unfamiliar road. I heard the sound of horses, and suddenly a troop of fifteen to twenty armed men rode around the corner at me. I was startled since I had never seen that sort of man before, but unfortunately not frightened enough to run into the thickest trees, where I might have escaped their reach. Instead I stood at the end of the path, staring at them in open-mouthed surprise as they approached.

In all of my nineteen years no one had ever warned me to be afraid of men coming here. Of course I had heard Marn's harsh accounts of things that happened "Outside," but that was far away, in another place. Our little settlement of women was deep in the woods. No men ever came there except to trade or to bring us unwanted girl-babies that we would raise as our own or to take away our boy children when they were old enough to leave for a new home. Such men were always friendly and respectful. They usually stayed awhile, taking a cup of tea with us, and sometimes a meal, and often sharing the gossip of other places, one of the few ways we got news of the outside world. In truth I knew little of the world of men. The settlement I lived in was part of the Women's Enclave, a network of towns, villages and settlements occupied only by women, existing under old agreements and having little to do with the rest of the world.

To my surprise the leader shouted at his men to grab me and I was instantly surrounded. At that moment I suddenly understood my danger and began, too late, to fight. I'm a strong woman, very strong, having done physical work all my life and also having walked miles in the woods, but I was not strong enough to ward off several men all intent on bringing me down. Yet even when they had my arms pinned I struggled, kicking out at them and trying my best to bite. Their leader strode up and slapped me back and forth across the face several times, not with evident anger, but with a cold, deliberate, measured intent.

No one had ever treated me that way. In my whole life no one had hit me. When he stepped back to stare at me, I stared back at him in shock, caught between fury and terror. He was indeed a frightening sight, a hulk of a man, tall and broad-shouldered, his dark good looks deeply tainted by cruelty.

"Stop fighting," he growled at me in a strange harsh voice that sent shivers up my back. "Do as you're told or you'll get more of the same and much worse. You're my captive now and you belong to me. My name is Peltron. Among these men my word is law. Remember that!" With that he began looking me up and down as if assessing what sort of creature he had captured. "What are you called?"

I clenched my teeth, not wanting to answer, but when he raised his hand to strike me again I muttered, "Solene," between swollen lips. After all, he already had my body. Why invite more hurt for something he would have from me sooner or later?

He gave me a grin that sent chills up my back. "Well, Solene, I think you will do nicely." Then he turned away and said to one of his men, "Gortal, take ten of your men and follow that path back. See where it leads and what else you can find. I have what I need for now. We'll go on and meet you back in the city."

Now my heart tightened with fear, not only for myself, but also for my family. What if they were able to follow my path back? Would they destroy our little village? Kill the people I loved? These men seemed so odd to me—almost not human—that I thought them capable of anything. Still I was given no time to linger there with my fears. My hands were quickly bound in front of me with a piece of rope. After that I was roughly lifted onto a horse led by one of Peltron's men, and the rope was tied to a loop on the saddle.

Almost immediately we began moving down the road. I glanced back in time to see some of the men turn onto the path I had just left. Soon we were around the bend. Everything familiar was gone and I was being taken away from the whole world I knew. I could feel blood running down my face and dripping from my chin. With my hands bound I couldn't even brush it away. No one around me noticed or seemed to care.

That night, when they camped, they untied my hands long enough for me to eat, giving me a bowl of scraps from their meal. All the while they joked with each other by making coarse, threatening, sexual comments, as if they wanted to misuse me in that way. Peltron didn't join in their talk. When it turned serious he told them harshly, "Don't think to touch her body in that way, any of you. Not on your life! You know she's for my brother." That stopped them, but as they glowered at me their silence seemed almost as threatening as their talk had been.

Afterward they bound my hands again and tied my feet to a tree. While the others slept, leaving just one guard awake, I leaned over as if I were dozing too, but actually I was chewing on the ropes that held my wrists. When I could tell by the sounds of his breathing that the guard was asleep, I broke through the last strands and swiftly untied my feet. Trying to make myself invisible I crawled toward the horses. When I thought I was far enough away I stood up and ran. I might have succeeded if I hadn't tripped over a branch and fallen. The branch broke with a loud snap. The men woke up and were on me in an instant.

When they had me pinned down, Peltron made the others back away. Then he tore my clothes and threw himself on me, violating me in my most private place that always before had been for pleasure. When he was done he stood up and said angrily, "I was going to save you for my brother, Torvin. Now, by your foolishness, you have forced me to do that. I told you that you were my captive, that I owned you. That was your punishment for trying to escape. There is more." With that he had me tied to a tree again and then beat me all over with a supple rod, especially on the bottom of my feet. I tried not to scream, but I almost fainted from the pain.

"That's so you won't try to run again," Peltron told me when he finished. "If you do I'll give you to my men and when they're done we'll leave you by the side of the road to rot." I had no doubt that he meant every word he said. He had the guard who fell asleep beaten almost as badly as he had beaten me. After that

I felt so hopeless I scarcely cared if I lived or died.

I think they must have drugged my water then, because the next days were all a blur. I know they tied me to the horse for the rest of the trip, but I hardly recall any of it. The first thing I remember clearly was the noise of the city cutting into my consciousness, so different from the sounds of home. It was like a constant roar, with many other sounds rising and falling within it and no silence anywhere. We stopped, surrounded by more buildings than I had ever seen in my life, and I heard Peltron bark out a series of harsh orders I could barely understand. Then one of his men rode up next to me and tied a cloth around my head, covering my eyes.

To the sound of hooves clopping on cobbles, we rode for a while through the city. Finally we stopped again. In pain, unable to see anything, unable to move my hands or feet, I sat there for several minutes, feeling utterly helpless and alone before I was roughly taken from the horse and carried into a building and up endless stairs. I was dizzy after a while with the many turns. The men who carried me groaned and swore under my weight and were none too gentle. This journey in darkness finally ended when they lowered me onto a bench and took off the blindfold. As soon as I could stop squinting against the light, I saw that I was in a well-furnished room almost as large as our whole house at home. Peltron was sitting in an enormous chair at the far end of it.

Before he presented me to his brother, Torvin, he had me unbound and brought before him. I couldn't stand on my own feet. The two men who had carried me in had to hold me up. Peltron looked me up and down in silence for a long moment, then said in his harsh voice, "Well, Solene, I captured you and brought you back here as a gift for my brother, who can find no woman in this city that pleases him. If you continue to fight with me I will have you killed right now and be done with it. You have already been far more trouble than you're worth. But if you decide to live, then you must be humble and pleasant and try in every way to please your new master."

The sound of Peltron's voice made my skin crawl. Already I despised this Torvin whom I had yet to meet. I could not imagine wanting to please the man. But I kept my eyes down in seeming humility and acquiescence, afraid Peltron would see the hatred blazing there. I was not, at that moment, ready to defy him.

After his little speech, Peltron called in some women who took me from his men and seated me in a chair. Making little murmurs of distress at the crusted blood everywhere, they cleaned me with soft cloths and a bowl of warm water. Next, with much effort, they brushed out my matted and tangled red hair that had not been tended since my capture. After that they dressed me in a fancy dress they couldn't fasten closed because of my injuries and put face paint over my bruises. They also put soft slippers on my damaged feet.

I kept flinching at their touch. They kept apologizing and glancing nervously at each other. Finally they set to arranging my hair, chatting as they worked. "Such fine hair." "Such an unusual color." "With a little twist like this we can make her look almost elegant." At last they fastened it up in a fancy coil and handed me the looking glass. Personally I would rather they had cut it all off and burned it. I had no wish for this sham of beauty.

When they were finished with me one of them whispered in my ear, "You are to be a Lanati. Your job is to please the man you are given to in every way." Later I understood that a Lanati was some combination of captive and whore, two concepts I had never encountered in my former life.

As soon as all the dressing and fussing was done with, Peltron called Torvin into the room. I looked over at this new tormentor, ready to hate the man. Instead I was surprised by his pleasant, gentle countenance. He looked like a younger, shorter version of his brother but with none of that cruelty in his face.

"Brother, I have brought you a gift," Peltron said grandly, gesturing at me. "This is Solene. She's full of spirit, very different from any of our women, a wild thing from the forest for you to tame. Look, she even has red hair so she must be the right one."

At the sight of me Torvin gasped and blushed a deep red. He

shook his head, looking far more shocked than pleased. "Brother, I thank you, but you shouldn't have. Sooner or later I would have found someone here."

"Well, if she doesn't please you she's headed for the slave pit or the market. That way at least I shall have some value from her."

Torvin recovered himself and said quickly, "No, no, she pleases me, she pleases me very much—though she hardly looks in need of taming."

Poor Torvin, I think it was pity that first bound him to me. If he refused this "gift" I was headed for a dreadful fate and somehow he would be at fault. I suppose he could see easily enough through the face paint and fine clothes how injured I really was. Indeed I couldn't walk without help. He had to support me out of the chair and down the hall. Whispering words of encouragement he brought me to this room, my lovely cage. Then, for the next week or two and with the help of Banya and Dorial—young women of about my age who were to become my gentle jailers as well as my maids and nurses—he slowly brought me back to health. During that time, against my will and in spite of all that had happened, I gradually grew to care for him.

It took a while for me to be able to stand on my own two feet. In the meantime I had to be helped from place to place. I was used to being strong and able, had never had a limp, had never even been sick, so I had little patience for this kind of care. I was probably a difficult patient. The healing seemed to take forever, but there finally came a morning when I could put weight on my feet without wincing in pain or needing assistance.

As soon as I could walk again the first thing I did was go to the window and look out. I could have had Dorial bring a chair over for me, but I wanted to be able to stand there on my own. From that spot I had a grand view of the city, all spread out below me, but the window, no doubt intentionally, was much too high for escape. Peering down into those unfamiliar streets I felt a sharp rush of loneliness and thought, *A city of strangers. Not one person out there that really knows me or loves me or cares whether I live or die.* In my home settlement of Nessian everyone knew me, had known me all my life. They knew my lover, my sister, my mother, my grandmother. They knew of my great-great-great-grandmothers who had helped to found our settlement. I had always lived in a tight, intimate web of connections, all of us woven together into the pattern of each other's lives. That was gone and I was alone now, alone as I had never been before in my life.

The room I was being held in was a lovely space, nothing to complain about there. It was large, gracious, sunny, beautifully furnished and full of things the like of which I had never seen before. Large luminous seashells—Torvin had to explain what they were and where they came from as I had never seen the sea and knew nothing of it. Tiny, intricate glass figures so fragile I was afraid to touch them. Silk cushions with elaborate embroideries of mythical creatures. Oil lamps in the shape of flying birds. I thought perhaps it had been furnished just for me, but Banya assured me it was just one of the many guest rooms in the Palace and that some of them were considerably more elegant.

Even now Banya sat in a sunny corner in a chair larger than she was, sewing and keeping watch on me, ready in an instant to fetch me anything I needed, but equally ready, I believe, to call a guard if I should try to escape. After all, her own life depended on keeping me there.

Banya and Dorial, my other keeper, were a strange contrast. Dorial was tall, wiry, broad-shouldered and very strong looking, with dark hair and swarthy skin. If I were running, wanting to get free, I imagined she could bring me down easily enough. She had grown up in the country and was not really comfortable in the city. "Not enough space here to stretch my legs—or my mind," she'd complain. "I wish I'd never come here." I could sense the discontent in her restless pent-up energy, though she was always kind enough to me.

Banya on the other hand was shorter, near my height, softer and rounder than Dorial, with pale skin, yellow hair and a sunny nature. She had been raised by her grandmother in a place she called "the hovels," a cluster of huts just outside the city gates, and she was quite content to be living in the Palace.

These two were my jailers, yet in spite of that we became friends of a sort, and in my loneliness I needed friends. When they brought me tea I invited them to share with me whatever was on the tray. At first Dorial would shake her head and look stern. And Banya would say, "We can't do that, Lady. It's forbidden." After a while they relaxed when they saw that only Torvin came to my room, and he certainly didn't care if we had tea together. He even seemed pleased to see me happy.

Ah, Torvin, what a strange relationship we had—or rather didn't have. What an odd dance we did together. I was supposed to be his Lanati, his sexual slave and he my master, yet it didn't seem to be that way at all. At first I was afraid of him, thinking he might use me roughly as his brother had, but I quickly lost my dread. In fact he seemed almost shy of me. Sometimes he would sit by me on the bed and put his arm around me, but if I stiffened or shivered he would instantly draw away. Finally he said, "I don't want to rush you, Solene. I hope you will come to me willingly and in your own time. I know my brother forced you and you are no doubt afraid. Trust me, I would never do such a thing. I only want to be gentle and kind and give you pleasure." This certainly didn't sound like a master.

Gradually I found my heart opening to him. Wavering between curiosity and wariness, attraction and aversion, I thought we might go further, become physical. I was even tempted, but in truth we never did more than exchange some fond hugs and a few experimental kisses. After one such exchange Torvin pulled away, cocked his head and looked at me, examining my face as if I were an interesting puzzle to be solved. "What is it about you? I have never felt these feelings for any woman before."

Nor I for any man, I was tempted to say, but I kept my silence for fear of where that would lead. Indeed I was surprised by the little thrills of excitement I felt from those kisses. But what Peltron had done to me had left me fearful. Dorial told me there was a name for that and it was called rape. What an ugly word. The very sound of it made me shudder.

"How could he do such a thing?" I had asked angrily, my voice full of outrage and indignation.

Dorial had shrugged and said in a hard, cold voice, "Happens more often then you might think." I wanted to ask if it had happened to her, but I didn't dare. The look on her face was too dark.

Though Torvin and I didn't proceed to being lovers, we did become fond companions. When he wasn't too busy helping his brother and father with the work of running the city he took me strolling through the Palace, showing me some of the endless wonders of the place—the paintings, the tapestries, the fountains, the glass-enclosed rooms full of plants, the elegant statues, the fish pond with bright golden fish flashing about and water lilies growing at the edges—room after room of dazzling surprises. Always a cheerful, friendly guide, Torvin was full of stories and information. He seemed to enjoy my company, except when I begged to go out into the streets. Then he would shake his head, look sad and say, "Later, not yet, Solene, not yet." And when he brought me back to my room he always made sure to lock the door if my young jailers weren't there to watch over me.

Because things between us were so deadly serious we almost never talked of significant things, keeping to a light and easy banter. But on one of our trips through the Palace, while Torvin was showing me some skilled carvings of wild animals done in black and red wood, he said with evident delight, "Beautiful, aren't they? Treasures brought back from a raid to the east."

"A raid?" I had been holding one of the carvings in my hands, caressing its smooth lustrous surface with pleasure. I almost dropped it. Instead I thrust it back into his hands, cold all over now, my pleasure gone in an instant. "What kind of raid?" I pictured people beaten or dead for these carvings and women raped.

He flushed and shook his head, realizing too late who he was talking to. After all, I was also a treasure brought back from a raid. I saw him struggling for words that would somehow mend the sudden rift between us.

I didn't wait. Now that he had opened that door I plunged through. "How is it that your brother came into the Women's Enclave with his armed men? I thought that was forbidden by binding agreements from ancient times, agreements that were made to last forever."

Now he looked even more uncomfortable, his kindly face tight with pain.

"Yes, those were the agreements, and they have held a long time, a very long time, but no agreements last forever. The truth is that everyone who made those agreements is dead and so are their grandchildren and great-grandchildren. Nothing lasts forever, not even the mountains, not even the rivers. Everything changes, Solene. Things are changing right now. Hernorium was just a town when those agreements were made. Now it is a city and growing fast. We keep pushing our boundaries. We have raided to the east and come up against the city of Kalthar. I suppose my father, as Magistrar of this city, is looking west or maybe my brother did this on his own. No one consulted me or I would have said not to do it. Peltron didn't even tell me what he planned. He said later he wanted to surprise me—which he surely did. In truth I think he didn't want to deal with my objections."

Torvin spoke as if he had had no part in all this and maybe that was the truth of it. He shook his head, looking troubled. "Perhaps my brother is trying to prove to our father that he can be a forceful leader so he will be chosen as successor instead of me."

"I thought the oldest son would naturally be chosen. I believe that's what Banya told me."

"I *am* the oldest son."

"Ah," I said in startled surprise. Turning to stare at him, I saw him flush again. "I thought you were the younger one." Even as I spoke, other questions quickly rose to mind. Was this some sort of rivalry between brothers in which I had been forced to play an unwilling part, much like the conflict I had with my sister Karil? Or was I nothing but a pebble tossed in a game of chance, a pebble on a much larger game board than I could begin to

11

comprehend? "You would be a much more suitable Magistrar. Peltron is a harsh, cruel man. You could make things better in this city."

"Make things better? How? What do you mean?"

"Many things. Slavery, for instance."

He took a step back and gave a strangled laugh. Fear flickered behind his eyes. "You think single-handed I could do away with slavery?"

"People love you, that's what Banya says."

"Ah yes, Banya. Banya doesn't know everything. How long would they love me if I told them their whole way of life was wrong?"

"But a man could..."

"Some man could—maybe, but not this man. Believe me, Solene, I'm neither a hero nor a fool. I know my limits. I'm not the man for that piece of work. In the first place I have no wish to be Magistrar and no skill for it."

I was about to say something more when Torvin's whole manner changed and his face suddenly shut down. "I should not be speaking to you of such things," he said abruptly. "It's not proper. After all, you're a Lanati." He had forgotten that for a while and treated me as a friend. We never spoke of serious things again.

With a sudden jolt I returned to the present and found myself staring out the tower window at this city that was my prison. As I watched some of the mist began to dissipate. The city was even noisier than usual with all the rush and bustle of making preparations for the Festival of Hern, the god for whom the city was named. Hernorium was built on the side of a hill and came down to the edge of the lake in a series of terraces. The Palace where my room was situated was high on the hill, and my window gave an excellent view of everything happening below. Ordinarily the gates that secured the Palace grounds were kept closed, but this morning, because of the festival and all the comings and goings that entailed, they were open and would be so all day. I gazed down at those open gates with such longing, such an intense desire to be free of this place, that it made my teeth ache and my throat go dry.

This Festival of Hern coincided to the day with our Midsummer's Day Gathering at home, our most important holiday, one that we celebrated with feasting and music and singing and dancing and visiting and the exchange of gifts, staying up all night around bonfires until dawn of the next day. I wondered if they would be celebrating today in spite of my absence. I knew my mother would be grieving. And likely others too. I knew from Banya that other women had been brought back by Peltron's men, though she had not yet been able to find out where they were from or what their names were.

Suddenly my thoughts flew back to my last day of freedom and the city with all its commotion faded away. That fateful morning I had quarreled one more time with my lover, Adana. We were following a familiar path of angry words that we had already traveled many times before. She wanted me to move away from our little settlement and go live with her in some larger place, anywhere—a bigger village, one of the two towns of the Women's Enclave or even a city "Outside." "I need someone with wider vision who can see beyond this narrow little world we were born into, someone with a sense of adventure. I'm smothering here."

How ironic that I was the one in the city, not Adana, though I doubt she would have liked it here. For me, I loved the fields and woods of home. I found enough adventure there, especially in the forest where every turn revealed something new. Just a few days before I was captured I had found a little spring-fed pond under huge old trees, surrounded by moss and ferns. I was careful to mark the way, thinking that I would bring Adana back there with me, a magic place for lovers. Now I understood that we would probably never go there together.

"I'm tired of you pulling on me," I had shouted angrily. "I don't want to leave. Go if you have to, but stop insulting me. I have my own adventures, adventures I find climbing a mountain or exploring a cave, and I'm tired of begging you to share them with me. Why don't you take Karil to the city with you? She'd follow you anywhere, a willing puppy. You have only to ask."

It was an unkind thing to say. My younger sister Karil envied me and yearned for anything I had, my red hair, my skill with horses, my lover. My lover most of all. She was always making eyes at Adana. She had long ago decided that our mother loved me best and was forever trying to find some compensation for it.

"I might just do that," Adana shot back.

"Good enough. I'm done with all this arguing," I had told her sharply. "I'm going to the woods to pick some mushrooms for the evening meal."

With that I had slammed out of my mother's house, where we had been living. That's what had begun the argument. I wanted us to start building our own house nearby, and she wanted us to leave together. I loved our settlement, loved everything about it. The way the hills curved protectively around our valley. The way the mist rose over the marshes with first dawn. The way the river shimmered blue and silver in the noon sun. The way our houses nestled in the hollow of the valley as if in the palm of a giant hand. It hurt me when Adana spoke disparagingly of this place that was so deeply part of my blood and bones, part of my own family's great adventure. My great-great-great-grandmother and her lover and their four daughters had started it, fleeing from abusive husbands and not wanting to settle in an already existing place where others might try to tell them what to do.

"You're a selfish fool," I had yelled to Adana as I stomped away. And she had shouted back, "And you're your mother's little baby, afraid to leave home."

Those were our last words to each other. Each time I thought of that I wished I could take back those words, at least mine. How little we know, how careless we are of the precious things in our lives. And now, with no explanation, I had disappeared from her world. And for all I knew she herself might be dead if Peltron's men had followed my tracks back to our settlement. How quickly

I would trade all the luxury in this room to hold Adana in my arms one more time, even if we had to part after that and go our separate ways. Was she still alive?

There was no one I could have asked, certainly not Peltron himself. *Did your men raid my village? Kill my mother? My lover? My sister? Burn down our home?* That was the first thing on my mind each morning when I woke and what I thought of every time I had a glimpse of that man in the halls of the Palace.

Of course I didn't dare ask Peltron such questions, but I did manage to ask Torvin about something that had been puzzling me. "What did Peltron mean about my red hair?"

He blushed slightly and looked embarrassed. "A month or so before he captured you I had a dream about a woman with red hair. She and I were sitting together on the mossy, fern-covered banks of a small, dark pond. It was deep in the forest. I told my brother about the dream, said that maybe that's who I was waiting for. Red hair is very rare among us so I thought it might stop him from pestering me about finding a woman that pleased me. Instead he found you."

A shiver ran up my back. It seemed as if Torvin had dreamt of my secret place in the woods. How was that possible?

"So it was my red hair that cost me my freedom," I said bitterly. Adana had always loved my red hair, petting and stroking it as if it might have a life of its own, separate from me. She liked holding it up to the sun "to see the fire in it." Gladly would I have cut it all off, shaved my head, to have avoided this fate. Thinking of my capture I pictured myself walking through the woods with all my angry thoughts directed toward Adana, dragging my mushroom sack, young and stupid and with no idea what was coming at me around the bend.

I was so lost in the past that Torvin slipped into the room without my even hearing him, unaware of his presence until he slid his arm around my waist, startling me out of my reverie. "It will be a beautiful day for the festival," he said eagerly.

"But it's so misty," I answered quickly, as if that mattered to me, as if that might not be even better for my purposes. "Will they still have the boat races?"

"Of course they'll have the boat races; they would have them even in the rain. Half the city has wagers on them. But I promise you, the mist will burn itself off soon enough, and the sun will shine through for the rest of the day. This is the biggest festival of the entire year. People will be pouring into the city from all around. They've already begun. The formal festivities are set to start at noon, first a soldiers' march for us to review and then horse races, boat races, foot races, wrestling matches, dance competitions, riding competitions, acrobatic displays, feasting, music, pig wrestling, even dogfights."

"Dog fights?" I exclaimed, turning to stare at him in shock. "What do you mean, dogfights?"

"Like dog fights on the street, only these dogs are trained for it, much stronger and fiercer. It's a bloody sport but very exciting. You'll see. My brother owns some of the dogs that will be fighting today."

Torvin spoke as if somehow I should care about his brother's interests, as if I were actually part of his family. I shivered. Peltron was a cruel man. I hated to think what he did to his dogs to make them eager to fight. Dogs in our village were gentle and friendly. The few fights that broke out were quickly settled. I couldn't imagine training dogs to fight—but then there was a good deal I couldn't have imagined before being brought here, starting with my capture and Peltron's violent treatment of me. Then a thought flashed through my head. I suddenly realized how I could use dog fights to my own advantage. My mind wandered off until I realized that Torvin was still speaking to me.

"...everything and anything you can imagine will be happening today, ending with a grand ball. And you will be here with me to enjoy it all. I have never before gone to the festival with a woman on my arm." He seemed oblivious of what it meant to me to be a captive and that I did not go with him of my own free will. And yet, at that moment, he sounded so much like a delighted and delightful boy it was hard not to love him—at least a little.

"Will you wear your new green dress?" he asked hopefully. He had brought me several dresses that I wore when we toured the Palace, but this new dress was his favorite.

I smiled at him, my heart aching with betrayal. "If it pleases you, I would be happy to do so."

With that he nodded and smiled back. "Yes, it pleases me very much. You're so beautiful in it, Solene, you'll be the envy of the whole city."

I thought that was not such a wise thing to be. Through Banya's gossip I already knew I had earned the hatred of Peltron's wife, Monice, by the unwanted accident of being more beautiful and getting far too much attention for it. I think Banya was proud for my sake, as if it reflected well on her, but it was certainly nothing I had ever cultivated or desired.

Torvin ran a tender hand down the side of my face and said wistfully, "You do love me, at least a little, don't you?"

I flushed. It was almost as if he had read my mind. "Of course I do. How could I not love a man who is so kind and gentle?" I spoke quickly, hiding my deeper lie with an easy truth, and felt again a sharp pang for the pain I would be causing him. Ah well, there was no help for it. I couldn't let it weaken my resolve.

"I'm hoping that I can get my brother and father to agree to our marriage—if that would please you."

Now my heart began pounding wildly, though I tried to keep my face rigidly composed. I knew I was blushing, but under the circumstances it might seem appropriate rather than suspicious. *Marriage? Marriage!* That was indeed the furthest thing from my mind.

"Of course it would please me," I answered quickly. "But perhaps not your brother—and certainly not his wife." Monice had given me hard looks and nakedly sharp words the few times we had passed each other in the Palace hallways. It seems that insulting a Lanati was fair game and not even considered rude in her circle. Other women were supposed to hate us if we were good at our work.

Torvin shook his head. "No matter. My father has long

wanted to see me married and making children. If I say I will marry no one but you he will have to finally agree. And if he does of course my brother will."

"This is a great honor," I said softly, making a slight bow so he couldn't see the expression of distress on my face. It was indeed an honor for a slave/whore to marry into the highest family in the city. Sometimes children of such unions were legitimized, fresh blood for the upper class, but such marriages were rare. All this was more information from the ever-talkative Banya.

"Banya, fetch your mistress her new dress and make her even lovelier than she already is."

After Torvin left, Banya and Dorial fussed over me for a long time. They would not allow me even a glimpse in the glass. When I was finally able to look into the mirror, the woman there was indeed beautiful. She was also, in a frightening way, a total stranger. Torvin had had me dressed up for show before, but nothing like this grand display. I, or rather she, had her red hair piled high on her head, curling about her forehead and falling softly around her face in tendrils and ringlets and tiny braids, all of this interwoven with jewels and ribbons and flowers. The silvery-green of the gown shimmered like sunlight on moss. The bodice of it made my breasts look fuller, and it was cut far lower than I was comfortable with here, much less in public. The gown came almost to my feet, which were encased in delicate matching green slippers, and the hem of it was gathered close at the ankles, making it difficult for me to take a long free stride.

Altogether the wares were elegantly displayed. "So beautiful, Torvin will be well pleased," Banya enthused. As I watched in the glass, a blush of shame and confusion rose in my already rouged cheeks. *A lovely helpless doll*, I thought as I stared at her. Dressed this way I couldn't climb out a window or run down the street or ride off on a horse—it was almost as good a restraint as ropes had been.

When Torvin came back, he smiled with pleasure and said gaily, "You will be the most beautiful woman there. Father will take one look at you and agree to anything."

"I can't run in such clothes or even walk fast," I grumbled ungratefully.

"Then you will have to hold onto my arm and hang on me. There's feasting this morning in the Great Hall before the festival. Everyone in the Palace will be there. I'm taking you now for a formal meeting with my father before we go to the reviewing stands." I shuddered inwardly. I would much rather not meet formally with his father. Indeed I dreaded it, but of course I had no choice in the matter.

The first time I had seen the Magistrar he had come into my room unannounced and ordered me to my feet. "Stand up and raise your arms. Now turn around slowly. Ah yes, good breasts, full hips, a fine figure and a pretty face. Peltron hunted well." I was afraid he was going to tell me to take off my clothes next. If he did, I wasn't sure what I would do. He even opened his mouth to say something more. Instead he shook his head and left abruptly. After he was gone, I sat on the bed shivering, and Banya had to hold me awhile to warm me up.

The next time I saw the Magistrar, he passed us in the Hall when Torvin and I were taking one of our walks. He was followed by several men I took to be his advisors, Peltron among them. Coming quite close, he leaned toward Torvin and said, "Well, boy, have you bedded her yet, or do you just enjoy parading her around the Palace?" Then, without waiting for an answer, he swept by with his entourage and left me burning with shame and anger.

The Great Hall was filled today with more people than I had seen in my whole life, and the noise was both deafening and frightening. I did indeed cling to Torvin's arm, at least for a while. The place was flooded with light from banks of tall, narrow windows, and the walls were lined with food-laden tables, more food, I think, than my whole settlement ate in a month. Bright tapestries hung all about the hall and a long red rug ran down the center of the floor. The Magistrar was seated at the back of the room on a high gold- and jewel-encrusted chair raised on a platform. People were moving forward slowly for an audience with him.

When he saw Torvin approaching with me on his arm, he made a wave of dismissal to the others, stood up, stepped down from the platform and took a few strides in our direction. The way quickly cleared between us. In a thunderous voice he said, "So this is the wild woman, your Lanati, and you are finally bringing her to meet me. About time. For an outlander, I must say, she dresses up quite nicely. Bring her forward."

The Magistrar was dressed in a robe of deep red, almost the same shade as the carpet, with several gold chains and medallions hanging around his neck. He had probably been as powerfully built as Peltron when he was younger, but it was clear he had let himself go to food and drink. He looked massive now, rather than strong. As Torvin brought me up to stand in front of him, I was aware of Peltron's wife, Monice, standing quite close and watching all this with a venomous look on her face as if she were envious of the attention. I would have been only too glad to give her my place in front of the Magistrar. "Yes, not bad looking, not bad at all," he continued, staring up and down my body as if I were naked and taking special interest in my scarcely hidden breasts. Then he ran his hand down my back in a slow intimate way that made my skin crawl. I shuddered and had to force myself to stand still, not jerk away.

Looking down so he couldn't see the flush of anger in my face, I pretended to be overcome with shyness as a cover for my lack of words. I was furious at that lecherous old man and even angrier at Torvin for his silence, for not protecting me. Who knows what dangerous things could have leapt out of my mouth if I had spoken at that moment. It was good that I didn't have a knife close at hand. I might have done some damage, and so ruined my chances for escape and probably ended my life.

"I hear there's some talk of marriage," the Magistrar went on. "Very irregular, of course, seldom done, but not altogether impossible. No, not impossible." The implication was clear, *Let me bed her and you can have her for your wife.* Then he waved us off.

20

"Go, go, eat, drink, make ready for the festival and show her off. I will finish with my duties here and see you in the stands."

We moved about the room, Torvin speaking and smiling, me nodding as if I were dumb of voice, people smiling at Torvin and greeting him, but openly staring at me and muttering as we passed. I heard the word "Lanati" several times and even the word "whore." I was deeply aware that in that city I had no real friend. Never in my life had I felt so uncomfortable or wished myself so strongly elsewhere. The room hummed with envy, malice, contempt and lust, all mixed in with a little pity. If I thought I had to remain among these people for the rest of my life I might really have killed myself or at least done something rash enough that they would have had to kill me, starting perhaps with bodily harm to the Magistrar. All of this was so far outside of my experience I could hardly grasp what was happening. If I could have run I might have done so, but my skirt was too tight around the ankles—and now I understood this was no accident. Today was the first time I was to be loose in the city and Torvin was taking no chances.

In the general hum of conversation I caught a few snatches now and then.

"...hear she's from far away. How did Peltron catch her?"

"...got her in a snare, the kind that's used for wild animals, for deer and foxes and the like."

"Quite right, and I know for a fact she tried to bite him when he was getting her leg free."

"...looks fairly civilized now."

"...Torvin, such a charming man, hope he gets some pleasure from her."

"Pity he couldn't have found someone here in the city."

"...trust he doesn't expect to bring her to my house for tea, though if he does of course I'll have to be polite."

"Wonder if she talks. Never heard her say a word."

"...have to admit she's pretty enough and that red hair is quite striking."

"Yes, but her skin's much too dark. Not even her fancy green

21

dress can hide that."

Of course I could talk—and I could also hear. *Do you think I'm deaf as well as dark-skinned?* I wanted to shout at them. I itched to tell that one woman, "Your skin is as pale as pastry dough and about as attractive. Mine is a lovely golden brown from the sun." In fact I longed to say things that were much ruder and angrier than that, but of course I kept my silence. I had more important things to deal with that day. If Torvin heard any of this, he wisely ignored it.

At some moment we passed quite close to Peltron and his wife, Monice of the angry countenance. She stepped forward to block my way. "Do you think to take my place here, Lanati? You'd best not give yourself airs. You know you could be in the slave pens tomorrow."

I had no idea how to give myself airs if I had wanted to or even what that meant. Peltron tugged sharply at her arm, "Come, Monice, no need for rudeness here."

He tried to sound stern, but there was a sly little smile on his face. I think he found this encounter amusing. No doubt he was enjoying both my embarrassment and his wife's frustrated anger. Perhaps he would have liked to pit us against each other in a pen. We could have been one of the events of the festival with everyone in the city making wagers. As I passed by, averting my eyes and making no answer, I could feel her stab of hatred in my back. Poor fool! Did she really think I wanted to be there?

A young man stood beside them who seemed like a thinner version of Peltron. He looked to be about seventeen or so, and he kept watching me with a strange hungry look on his face, a sort of mixture of lust and contempt. As we moved away from them, I drew Torvin toward me and whispered to him, "Who is that? I don't like the way he's looking at me."

He knew instantly who I meant and whispered back, "That's Peltron and Monice's son, my charming nephew, Ramule. Pay him no mind. He's just jealous that his father didn't bring you back for him." I felt a shudder of revulsion at those words and renewed my resolve to escape that day.

22

Torvin kept urging me to eat, but I had no appetite, especially after that encounter. "I'm too excited right now," I told him. "Perhaps I'll eat some later."

It seemed such a shame, such a waste, that this vast glut of food would be here now, heaped on the platters and covering all the tables, when I didn't even want it. Later, when I would be really hungry, there would be nothing. With that in mind I gathered a little food for my escape, wrapping things in a napkin and putting the napkin in the green embroidered bag that swung by a silk cord at my wrist and matched my lovely dress. Later the bag would be soiled and greasy, but in the sum of things that hardly mattered.

As we were leaving, I couldn't help myself. I leaned close to Torvin and hissed angrily in his ear, "You let your father put his hands on me and you said nothing!"

"Ah, Solene, what does it matter? He's an old man and harmless, only looking for a little warmth. Ever since my mother died he's been lonely." And I was already soiled goods so why not? What harm? I could well imagine how many young women got fed to that man's loneliness, but I shrugged and said nothing more. Just one more reason to be gone.

Before we left the Palace Torvin told Dorial she could have a few hours off to go to the festival if she wanted. He even put some coins in her hand. "But be back in the early afternoon in case Solene should need you. We may not stay very long since this is her first day out." Banya we took with us, to be my maid and help me in any way she might be needed.

When we stepped out through the great arched doors that opened into the cobbled courtyard, Torvin gave me his arm to help me into a waiting carriage. "Wait," I said quickly. "I never saw the Palace from the outside. After all, I was brought here blindfolded." I saw a quick flash of pain cross his face and knew that out of guilt he would grant me almost anything I wanted. He nodded. I took his arm and he led me out from under the protection of the stone archway to where I could look up and see the Palace. It was huge, much bigger than I had imagined from the inside and composed of three parts, the central tower that held my room and two matching wings.

The tower itself was built of enormous blocks of dark rough-cut gray stone with no ornamentation to relieve its harshness except some carvings around the doors and windows. It was probably ten or twelve stories high and looked ancient and impregnable, as if built for defense. I thought it could easily have sheltered a whole village or maybe even a town inside its walls. The wings, in contrast, were lower, four or five stories at the most, and appeared to be much more recent. They were built of bands of different colored stones, decorated with elaborate carvings and intricate patterns of bright tiles. The doorway we had come through was the entrance into the right-hand wing and I could see the long windows of the Great Hall just above. Across from us was a long, low building that I took to be the stables, as horses were constantly being led in and out. Scattered around the courtyard were many more buildings whose uses I couldn't even guess at, a whole little village inside the city, surrounded by a stone wall the height of two men and guarded by the great wooden gates that today stood open.

"Tell me about it," I asked Torvin, hoping for as much time as possible to look around and mark the location of everything. "The tower looks very old."

"The tower was built when we thought there was going to be a war with Kalthar. Before that there had been a much smaller stone building on that spot. The war never materialized, perhaps because of the tower, but that was the start of the Palace. My great-grandfather built the opposite wing and my great-grandmother chose the tiles. She came here as a young bride and she is supposed to have said, 'I refuse to live in this dungeon, I must have some color around me.' My grandfather started this wing with the Great Hall you were in this morning and my father finished it."

Torvin seemed quite proud of the Palace. I thought the tower ugly and forbidding, but I had to admit that the bands of stone on the new wings were handsome, and the brightly colored tiles

24

were beautiful. Still, it was hard to admire my prison.

"Where is the entrance where I was brought in?"

"The doorway at the base of the tower, the one you can see from here. The doorway leading to the kitchen is just around the corner."

And right opposite the stable entrance, as I was glad to see. I thought I had asked enough questions and tarried long enough. I didn't want to make Torvin suspicious. I slipped my arm through his and said with a gaiety I didn't really feel, "On to the festival."

We went by carriage to stone viewing stands that lined one side of a grand avenue. I stared out the window at everything, turning my head this way and that, trying to see it all so I could better understand this place I would try to escape from later. Hernorium seemed large, crowded, noisy, confusing and altogether far more frightening down here on the ground than it had from my window perch high above the streets. I could feel my resolve weakening. Afraid I couldn't manage to find my way out, I had to keep repeating to myself, *dead or gone, dead or gone by day's end*, as though I wasn't afraid and it didn't really matter which one.

The royal section of the stands was at the center. Peltron and Monice were already in their seats. Monice's maid, Vonga, was sitting beside her on one side and Ramule on the other. Peltron sat next to his son, who was looking sullen and bored to distraction. I thought from Ramule's posture that he might be in some silent struggle with his parents. Perhaps he would rather have been walking around the festival with his friends, pinching girls and making wagers on the boat races, not stuck that way between them, a book trapped between two stiff bookends. He was mostly silent, mumbling answers only when spoken to. I was glad that after one quick glance our way he totally ignored me.

People immediately made way for us. Torvin sat next to Peltron with me on his other side and then Banya next to me. Even with Torvin between us I could still feel Peltron's threatening presence. We were no sooner seated than there was a blare of trumpets, a roll of drums and the Magistrar took his place in a high seat right behind us. He was accompanied by several older men who were probably his councillors. The hair on the back of my neck went up. Even though he was seated directly behind Peltron, he was much too close for my liking.

There was a noisy chatter in the stands. I stared about me, observing everything while trying not to look too curious. After a while music could be heard gathering in the distance and then the thunder of marching feet. Gradually people fell silent and in that silence I clearly heard Monice's aggrieved voice. "It's not right that she should be sitting here on my level. It's shameful and it hurts my dignity. Let her sit down on one of the lower rows with the other Lanati or down on the wooden benches by the street. That's where she belongs."

I started to rise, only too happy to go elsewhere, but the Magistrar reached forward and clamped a powerful hand on my shoulder. "Stay where you are," he said harshly. Then to Monice he added, "Enough of your troublemaking, Monice. I say where people sit, not you. I order you to restrain your mouth and your jealousy for the remainder of this day."

Now, of course, everyone in the stands turned to stare at this delightful and unexpected show. I blushed uncomfortably and again wished myself elsewhere. The stares did not last long, however, because soon enough the musicians and the marching men came into view and all attention turned back in that direction. The soldiers came, row after row of them, on foot, on horseback, with swords and shields, with bows and arrows, with spears—an impressive and thoroughly terrifying sight. Who could ever stand up against such a force? It would roll over anyone foolish enough to try, like a giant chariot of annihilation. I grew sick and numb, watching this river of death that flowed on and on before us, with sunlight flashing brightly on all that metal.

Finally the parade was over and we were able to leave. I was only too glad to be away from Peltron and his poisonous wife and his sullen son and especially to be away from the Magistrar with his heavy hand, though I understood that we would all assemble again for the boat races. Torvin asked me if I felt well enough to walk or if I preferred the carriage. Of course I chose to walk and for a little while I had an illusion of freedom, strolling along on Torvin's arm, with Banya beside me. Though I was always conscious of Torvin's men following us, they stayed back out of sight and did not intrude. Torvin even gave me a few coins to spend and I bought a paper twist of sweets. I shared some and stuffed the rest into my green bag for later, covering the food I had already stashed away.

Wherever we went, the way always parted respectfully for us, and whenever we chose to stop and watch some event people quickly moved aside so we could see. We were entertained by acrobats and jugglers, dancers and fancy riders, all in bright colorful costumes. We watched all sorts of trained animals doing unbelievable tricks. We walked through markets with amazing goods for sale, many of them things I had never seen before. Viewing all this, I began to have some concept of why Adana had wanted to live in a town or a city, what she was looking for, the richness and excitement and variety that was possible.

Torvin bought a pastry for me, another for himself and also one for Banya. For a while we walked along together munching and talking, exclaiming over the sights and pointing things out to each other as if—at least for that moment—we really were just three friends out enjoying the day and each other's company. I noticed that Torvin treated Banya with kindness and consideration even though she was just a servant, not much more than a slave really, very different from the way I imagined Monice treated her maid.

After a while we came to a part of the market where they sold beautifully colored birds in cages, row upon row of cages stacked on each other everywhere I looked. Seeing the birds fluttering about, trapped and helpless, tears stung my eyes and my heart contracted. I remembered again that I was a Lanati and not a free woman out for a day's pleasure. Torvin asked me if I would like a bird to keep me company in my room. I could not imagine wanting to keep a bird trapped in a cage. I shook my head, afraid to look at him, picturing the birds that used to gather on my mother's windowsill to eat the seeds we left there for them. I wondered if they still gathered there, chirping happily, unaware of my plight, free to fly away at will. I wondered if my mother's house was still standing, if she was still alive, missing me, crying and wondering where I had gone, or if she herself was dead. Before my capture, we had seldom spent a whole day apart.

My tears in danger of spilling over, I tugged on Torvin's arm, wanting to be gone from there. After that we strolled by a pond and watched the ducks and swans, stopped to listen to some music and saw the end of a puppet show, but I never regained my momentary illusion of well-being. All too soon the trumpets blew for the boat races and we turned our steps toward the lake.

The stands there were wooden and temporary, very different from the formal, stone viewing-platform on the avenue. This time, when we were seated, I noticed Ramule was absent, probably watching from somewhere else with his friends. I was also very relieved that the Magistrar and his companions were not there. I was afraid they might arrive at any moment, but the royal seats behind us remained empty.

In spite of everything I was struck by the beauty of the scene— the sun gleaming on the water, the multicolored banners flapping and snapping in the breeze, the parade of elegantly decked riders trotting their horses along the edge of the lake, the constant flow of people in their finest clothes, the sight of the boats themselves. The racing boats were long and narrow, brightly painted, with the bows carved in the shape of fierce, fanciful animal heads, each different from all the others. There was a crew of twenty oarsmen to a boat, ten on each side, a drummer to keep time seated at the front, a steersman at the back and a man with a whip standing just in front of him. We watched as they rowed up and down, warming their well-oiled muscles in the sun and getting ready for the races.

As the first race was about to begin, Torvin leaned close and said in my ear, "Keep a close eye on the red and gold boat. We have a wager on it."

"You and your brother?"

"No, you and I. If we win, I will split it with you and you can spend yours in the market for whatever you want. My brother's bet is on the blue and black one. Those are his colors. He owns it."

"And you own the red and gold one?"

He nodded and I thought, *and probably all the men in it as well.*

When the race began, I actually found myself leaning forward eagerly, willing "our" boat to win, wanting, needing the money, hoping I could set some aside for my escape. At first the sound of the drums, the whips, the paddles, the groans and shouts of the men came clearly across the sparkling water. Then the shouts and cries from all around me drowned out everything else. The stands were actually shaking from everyone's eager frenzy. For just a moment several boats seemed to be racing almost together and it was impossible to tell who had the advantage. Then a black and silver boat pulled ahead of the others. There was a great shout as it passed first between the signal flags planted in the water. I sat back with a sigh, ashamed to have been caught up so intently in a race where slaves were being beaten to win. I heard Peltron on the other side say angrily, "I think my boatman is too light-handed with his whip. I don't like to lose. I'll have to speak to the man."

Torvin shrugged and said casually, "Well, we didn't win either." Then he turned to me. "You didn't really care, did you?"

I shook my head and turned away so he wouldn't see my tears of disappointment.

There were several more races in which none of this company had wagers. I began to lose interest in the scene and wished we were walking about again. I was about to suggest it to Torvin when Peltron leaned over to him and said abruptly, "I need to talk to you alone, Brother, before anything else gets said this day about marriage. We need to clarify some things." His words had an ominous tone, as if he had been sitting there all this while, thinking troubled, angry thoughts. Torvin turned to me and said quickly, "Stay right there, Solene. I'll be back soon." *As if I was free to go anywhere else.*

29

When they got up to go, I was left sitting in the same row as my enemy and with no one between us. I wondered if that had been the intention of that abrupt departure. Quickly I signaled Banya to come sit between us. Before she could move Monice raised her hand with some money in it. "Banya, you and Vonga go buy yourselves some custards at the bakery stall in the River Street market—and don't hurry back."

Banya hesitated, glancing anxiously at me. With a nod I signaled her to leave. What else could I do? I couldn't openly oppose Monice. She outranked me in every way and in that world rank meant everything. I braced myself, wondering if she meant to do me actual bodily harm and if she did what I could do to protect myself that wouldn't mean my death or worse.

No doubt seeing the fear in my face she said quickly, "You're safe, Solene. I just need to talk to you and it needs to be very private." With that she moved over next to me and leaned close to my ear. Now I had no way of escaping her. When she went on it was almost as if to herself and she appeared very agitated.

"The fool! Why did he have to do it, go and find Torvin a woman? It was fine by me that Torvin had no wife and no children. Children are heirs. Didn't he think about Ramule? Didn't he even care about his own son who would make a much better Magistrar than either Peltron or his father? The boy should have his chance. If Torvin has children, the city might well pass into their hands. Torvin is the old man's favorite. And besides, why should Torvin have a choice of mate when none of the rest of us did? His father should just have chosen a suitable wife for him and not indulged him so." When she stopped at last she was staring at me or rather through me with frightening intensity, almost as if she didn't see me at all.

I wanted to assure her that she had nothing to fear on that account. Torvin would certainly not be having any children with me. Then I thought it was probably wiser not to speak on the matter. Finally, after a long strained silence, I asked, almost in a whisper, "What do you want from me, Monice?"

At that she seemed to come back to herself and said again,

with even more urgency this time, "I need to talk to you."

"You hate me, Monice. Why would you want to talk to me except to do me harm?"

"You need to hear me out. Whether I hate you or not doesn't matter. It is of no importance. What matters is that I'm willing to help you. Are you thinking to do it today in the confusion of the festival?"

"You know nothing about me," I told her emphatically, feeling both frightened and angry now. "Nothing! We come from very different worlds."

"I know what I know because we are both women. I know you have no intention of marrying Torvin and living in this city."

"You know nothing about me!" I said again. And then I sighed and shrugged, giving up the struggle. I had said to myself that morning *dead or gone by day's end* and now it looked more like dead. "Do you plan to betray me as soon as they come back, or will you shout now for one of your husband's men?"

"What a fool you are! Aren't you listening to me at all? Don't you hear what I'm saying? I have no intention of betraying you. I want you gone from here as much as you want to go. And I don't want you caught and tortured and lingering about in the dungeon, drawing attention to yourself and disrupting my life in the city. I want to help you leave."

"How did you know?"

"I told you, because we're both women and women in this city have no power. Anything we want we have to get by subterfuge and trickery. I've puzzled about it all day and now I understand. If you had wanted to marry Torvin, you would have flirted with his father, tried to charm him, taken advantage of all the chances you were given—and you were given many this morning, none of which you took. Marriage is the best opportunity for a Lanati. It guarantees your safety. It can keep you out of the slave pens when you're older. And Torvin is the best possible man to marry—so instead you must be planning to escape—and I plan on helping you."

"How can I trust you? Why should I?"

31

"Just think about what I said, then you'll know." I looked at her for a long thoughtful moment, staring into her eyes while she looked steadily back at me. Then I gave her a little nod and she went on. "Now we must talk quickly before any of them come back. I have a little money I can give you, not much but enough to get you home, but you must hide it where no one will look. And I have a horse in the Palace stable. She's being kept saddled for me this afternoon in case I want to take a turn around the park. She's not showy, not easy to spot, not even very fast, but steady and reliable. No one will miss her if I say nothing. They'll think she's with me. She has a white star on her forehead and one white sock. Darken the white with boot polish, rough up my fancy saddle and no one will stop you. Or if you're spotted just say you're bringing her to me at the festival grounds. If you take any other horse someone will be sure to miss it and raise a cry.

"You'll need a good start if they decide to give chase, hopefully some part of this afternoon and all of tonight. One thing is sure, I don't want you to stay here and marry Torvin and have a litter of pretty little children, find favor with the Magistrar, push me and my son out and perhaps even spoil my husband's chance of becoming Magistrar when his time comes. He has a right to that." Her words all came out in a frenzied rush.

I looked at her in amazement. "Do you love him that much?"

Now it was her turn to be amazed. She turned her head to stare at me. "Love? This has nothing to do with love. He's a good husband and a good father to our son. He doesn't beat me much; he gives me whatever I need. He deserves to be Magistrar, though his father favors Torvin because he's 'so charming.' Peltron didn't think of what he was doing to his own chances by dragging you back here, but he cares for his brother and wanted to make him happy. Now I think he's already regretting it. He hadn't planned on marriage, only on finding a woman Torvin could bed and find some pleasure with for a year or so, even a month or so before he discarded her."

Now I was staring back at her, eyes wide. "But Peltron is a terrible man. He raped me and beat me. He beat the bottom of

32

my feet so that I couldn't even walk."

She shrugged and her face turned hard. "So what is that to me? He does many terrible things in the course of helping to run the city. As long as he treats me well, I don't question him. That's not my business. I'm only the wife promised to him at thirteen, married at sixteen. Do you think I had any choice in the matter? Torvin has done terrible things too. Do you think him so different because he smiles and acts kind? Don't be so easily fooled. Now we must be quick. They'll be back soon. Here's the money. Slip it into your bodice.

"My horse is in the third stall at the back row of the stable. If my husband finds out I have helped you he'll probably kill me for it, so get yourself gone from here and don't get caught. Take Lake Street down the hill and out through the Westgate of the city, then the central cobbled road to the Westway. That's the best way to get past the farmland and back into the forest. After that you're on your own. I know nothing more. I've never been that far away. Go west from here, keeping the sun at your back in the morning and in your face in the afternoon. If they catch you, don't say I had any part in this. It would mean my life."

She slipped me the money in a tiny drawstring pouch that I quickly hid away in the bodice of my dress. At that moment there was a commotion in the stands. I glanced up just in time to see that one of the boats was close to tipping over as it turned to come back in our direction. The shouts and cheers from the stands and the crowd down below grew even louder as the boat wobbled precariously and then finally righted itself. "Can they all swim?" I asked Monice anxiously.

She shrugged again. "It matters little one way or the other. They're chained to the boat. If the boat goes over they drown. It's considered a sacrifice to Hern, God of weather and water for whom this city is named. Good luck for us if men drown at His festival. We feed Him and He feeds us in return, bringing us good crops that year. That's why people were cheering."

Horrified, I stared at her in disbelief for a long moment—then turned away. I could not imagine people worshipping a god who feasted on drowned men. In the Women's Enclave our deity was Evandaru, Mother of all, Goddess of the seasons, the crops and childbirth. She had guided us to the enclave, nurtured us and watched over us through all our struggles there. The only offerings we made Her were a plate of food on her altar at feast time, some fruit and vegetables at harvest time and flowers all the time, flowers from field or garden as long as the season held. She asked for no sacrifice of human or creature. After all, She was the Mother of all things. I don't know if I really believed in Her or not, but the thought of Her was comforting nonetheless, something to hold on to in hard times, though I had not found Her much help in Hernorium. Here my pleas to Her were met with silence. Still the statue of Her in Nessian was beautiful, and I loved the chants we all sang in Her honor.

I couldn't look at Monice anymore, so I sat there deep in thought, wondering whether cruel men created a cruel God to justify their actions or whether a cruel God created cruel men in His image. After giving me the money, Monice had moved back to her own place. With nothing left to say, we each sat in tense silence. I was renewing my vow to myself, *dead or gone by day's end*. I had to go home. No way could I live among these people. When I was sure Monice's attention was elsewhere I shifted the money pouch to my green bag, concealing it under the paper twist of sweets.

My mind spinning with all she had told me, I finally glanced at Monice a few times. She sat staring straight ahead and seemed to have forgotten my presence. Soon Banya and Vonga came back, each with a bag of sweets. Banya offered me some, but I shook my head. Shortly after that the men returned, seeming in a much better mood. Peltron grinned at his wife and said, "Well, I see you have not attacked each other while we were gone."

"I thought it better if we made peace. It would not do to have your father angry at me."

"Good choice," he said with a harsh laugh, as he took his seat. To my surprise he even bent to give her a quick kiss.

Another race passed before our eyes, but I had no more

interest in the scene. Then there were loud screams and shouts from behind us, and Peltron said eagerly, "The dogfights have started. Enough of this boat racing; it grows tiresome. I have a dog in the fourth fight."

Torvin turned to me. "Do you wish to go or stay?"

This was what I had been dreading and waiting for all day. Not wishing to seem too eager, I shrugged and said as casually as I could manage, "We may as well move on and see something new." When I glanced at Banya I saw a look of deep distress on her face, but I said nothing. No matter, she was my maid, the slave's slave, and she would have to go with me whether she liked it or not.

This event was being watched at street level. When we reached the ring, people made way for us again. Someone quickly offered me a chair, but I refused. A chair did not suit my plans. "Are you sure?" Torvin asked me solicitously. "This has been a long day for you."

"Quite sure. I can see much better standing. I've never watched a dogfight before." Just as we got there something dark and bloody was being dragged away. I tried not to look at it. Sawdust was immediately scattered around the ring. It quickly turned red and was swept into a pile at the edge. On one side of the ring I saw an area reserved for the dog cages and handlers. People crowded the rest of the circle, pushing in to get a better view. The noise around us was deafening, the whole place a pandemonium of growls, barks, howls and shouts, with dogs flinging themselves against their cages and bets being called out back and forth across the ring.

As we watched two dogs were brought out and displayed to the cheering, jeering crowd. They lunged forward, barking furiously, trying to get at each other while their handlers dug in their heels to hold them back. Their names were called out, and the betting grew even more frenzied. One of the dogs was brown and white, bigger than its opponent, but the other, a black dog, had broader shoulders and a wider head. Both of them baring their teeth and snarling, seeming ready to kill. To me they hardly looked like dogs, certainly not like the ones I knew from home.

At a signal both dogs were released. They flew at each other in a fury, becoming a snarling, heaving mass that quickly turned bloody. Flinging themselves from one side of the ring to the other, they each struggled to get the advantage. Very soon it became clear that the black dog was winning. I expected them to stop the fight and allow the brown and white one to escape, but apparently this was not to be. With a last fierce growl the black dog grabbed the other dog's face in his jaws, ripped off its ear and part of its cheek. At that there were excited blood-screams from all around me, and I had no difficulty faking a faint. Giving a cry of horror, I collapsed right into Torvin's arms. Before I shut my eyes, I saw blood spatter across my new green dress.

Torvin immediately lifted me away from the ring, calling for his men. With their help I was quickly carried to the carriage. The horses were whipped into a run as we rushed to the Palace. Once there I was carried to my room and laid on the bed. With Banya's and Dorial's help Torvin stripped off my fancy clothes, dressed me in my nightdress and covered me with a quilt. At that point I pretended to slowly and painfully come back to consciousness. "Where am I? What happened?" I asked in a dazed, bewildered voice, tossing my head back and forth in distress.

Torvin took my hand. "You fainted at the dogfights. You said it was your first time. It can be hard if you're not used to such sights." Then he pulled a chair up by the bed and said with concern, "I'll sit here by you until you're better. I had so hoped to dance with you tonight at the ball."

I shook my head. That was certainly not part of my plan. "No, please, you must go back to the festival. Your people need to see you on such an important day. I'm going to sleep for the rest of the afternoon and probably right through the night. I would feel very badly to have spoiled your pleasure. Besides, there's no way I can dance on these sore feet. I walked on them far too much today."

"I'm afraid it was the dogfight that…"

"Best not to speak of it," I said with a shudder. "I'll be seeing that horror in my head for a long time to come." When he still hesitated, I said, "Please, Torvin, it will only make me anxious to have you hovering about here and serve no good purpose. It may even make it hard for me to sleep if I'm worried for you. I suppose I did too much this first day out, but now a good night's rest will mend me right enough. Banya and Dorial will be right here if I should need anything."

"I'll be back this evening to see how you're doing."

"Not this evening," I said quickly—perhaps too quickly. "I plan to sleep the sleep of the dead tonight and wish not to be disturbed." I held my breath, afraid I had been too forward, the slave dictating to the master. To seal the matter I beckoned him to me, signaled that he should bend forward and kissed him full on the lips for a long moment—my kiss of betrayal. It hurt to see the look of pleasure on his face when he stepped back. "Come tomorrow morning, Torvin, but not too early. I will be well again by then and glad to see you."

He left with obvious reluctance and I trembled to think he might come back again for one last look. Meanwhile Banya began gathering up my soiled green dress from the floor with a mournful look on her face, almost as if she was grieving for it. "It was so beautiful, and you looked so lovely in it, and now it's all ruined," she said sadly.

I laughed with a gaiety I certainly didn't feel. "No use to cry over that one, Banya. If it can't be cleaned and mended, Torvin will have a new one made for me. Now, if you would pass me my little embroidered bag I think I still have some sweets from the market in it." I had dropped the embroidered bag into the folds of the dress as they stripped me for bed. I cared not one bit for that dress that had hobbled me all day. In fact I was glad to be shed of it, but I wanted my green bag safely in my hands. As soon as I had hold of it I took out the paper twist of sweets, shared them around and put the rest back. Then I slipped the green bag under my pillow with an inward sigh of relief. My stash was safe, at least for that moment.

37

While I waited to put my plans in motion, I asked Banya and Dorial to take down my hair and dress it in a braid for the night. A single braid would best serve my purpose. When Dorial came near me I thought she smelled of drink. She seemed not quite steady on her feet, and her hands, as she worked on my hair, shook slightly. She must have been celebrating hard at the festival in the short time she was there, with most of the coins Torvin had given her going to drink rather than food. I said nothing on the matter, but thought it served my purpose well for her to be less than sober. I hoped Torvin hadn't noticed. Banya also said nothing, though surely she must have been aware.

As they worked, they chatted with each other about the events of the day, comparing what they had seen. They were no longer stiff and wary with me as they had been at first but spoke easily in my presence. Listening to them, I thought how much they sounded like girls from home and how much I liked them both. Now I was about to use them in a way that might well cost their lives. I felt the guilt of it bite into me but not enough to turn back. There would never be another chance like this. *Gone or dead by day's end*, I told myself again, saying it over and over in my mind to harden my resolve.

When I was quite sure Torvin was really gone and not likely to come back, I said to Banya, as if on sudden inspiration, "Just a few more tasks, then I'll let you go home to visit with your grandmother. After what happened today I plan to sleep like a log so you need not be back until morning."

Next I asked Dorial to sit outside my room in a chair and guard the door so no one would bother me. Looking pleased, she nodded and left. In her condition I thought she would be glad to just to stay in one place and not be running around waiting on me. Besides, I needed her out of my room.

After that I sent Banya to fetch some tea. "The kind that is soothing and will help me sleep. Though I'm exhausted I'm also very agitated from all I've seen. And bring a second cup for yourself and maybe some little cakes as well."

It was my habit to share tea with them so this wouldn't seem strange. While Banya was gone I went on quick, silent feet to fetch the sleeping draught that Torvin had given me when I was hurting so badly all over that I couldn't sleep. He had warned me of the dangers of taking too much but had been careless enough to leave it in the cupboard. By the time Banya returned I was back in bed, ready for her, the bottle safely hidden under my pillow. She poured out both cups of tea and arranged some little cakes on a plate.

"Banya, would you get me another pillow from the couch and also my robe and slippers from the wardrobe and another cover please from the chest? I think I got a chill today." I hoped all that would take long enough to give me the time I needed. Instantly she turned her back and busied herself with attending to my requests. While all her attention was elsewhere, I added a good dose of the draught to her cup and quickly stirred it. In my nervousness I dripped some on the table. Hoping she wouldn't notice, I wiped at the droplets with my sleeve.

When she had fetched everything I asked for and had propped me up in bed with the extra pillow behind me, we drank our tea in companionable silence. It had been a long day and I was fighting sleep myself. Finally Banya said, "I thank you more than I can say for sending me home to my grandmother. She's getting old and has not been well. She raised me, you know, saved me from my drunken mother when I was just a baby. I wouldn't be here now if not for her."

That nearly undid me. I could hardly bring myself to answer and had a moment of almost blurting out the truth. Instead I took a deep breath to calm myself and said, "I understand. I also had a grandmother I loved very much. She's dead now, but I think of her often." All lies. In truth my grandmother had been an ill-tempered woman who had caused my mother much misery before she died of a snakebite when I was twelve. I had always blamed her for the departure of my mother's companion, my second mother, Marn. Amazing that I had learned to lie so quickly and become so skilled at it. All the time I was growing up I had never lied. There was no need to with a mother who was kind and caring and adored me as a gift in her life. It seemed that in this city every few words out of my mouth were lies.

Banya, now that the silence was broken, set herself to prattling on and on about the day's events as if she were becoming more animated instead of sleepier. I kept watching her eyes for signs of drooping and quickly went from worrying that I had given her too much to being sure it had not been enough and my chances were now spoiled. I wasn't ready for it when she gave a sudden nod, her eyes rolled back in her head and she toppled forward, crashing against the tea tray with a loud sound of breaking china.

I heard Dorial call out anxiously, "What's wrong? Is something wrong?"

Afraid she would come bursting in and ruin everything, I answered quickly, "Nothing's wrong. All's well. Just my clumsiness. I stumbled against the tea table. I'm going to bed before I do any more damage. Banya's leaving soon and I'll probably sleep through till tomorrow." I was trying to sound calm and reassuring, but my heart was pounding, my hands sweating and shaking.

Quickly I put a palm over Banya's nose, relieved to feel the warm breath there. I was afraid I had misjudged the dose. Though her breathing seemed shallow, she was very much alive and totally unconscious. Now I had to move a sleeping body all by myself and do it without sighing or groaning with effort. I had never realized how heavy a body could be. First I tipped her back in the chair, propping her there with a pillow so I could get the tea table out of my way and avoid any more noisy crashes. That done, I began to pull off her clothes. They were valuable to me now in a way no fine gown could possibly be. It was a terrible struggle, her arms feeling as heavy as bedposts and as limp as bread dough. It was as if she were fighting me in her unconscious state.

Once I had her clothes free of her limp form, I stripped off my own nightgown. Dressing her in it, working her arms into the sleeves and the rest of it down around her body, was almost as hard as taking her clothes off had been. Next came the task of slipping her out of the chair and over to the bed, luckily only a short distance, but again with the need for total silence. By the time I hauled my limp burden to the bed I was exhausted. Now I had to actually get her in the bed. I didn't think I could do it alone. I sat down next to Banya's still form and wept silently, leaning my head against her shoulder. It was time to admit I had failed.

After a few moments of this, my will reasserted itself. *Dead or gone by day's end*, I reminded myself. I got Banya into a sitting position, leaned her against the bed and with supreme effort pushed her up and over the edge. She almost flopped back. I caught her just in time and rolled her over to the middle of the bed.

Now I had to hurry. The sooner I was done here the sooner I could be away, gone before my absence was discovered. I took Banya's scissors from her sewing basket and cut off my braid, hacking through the thick hair with effort. Then, taking some brown boot polish from the cupboard, I brushed it into my hair to cover the red and even smudged some on my face. I looked terrible, but it certainly changed my appearance. Dressed in Banya's clothes, with a blouse and skirt of plain brown homespun and her scarf tied over my greasy hair, I looked at myself in the mirror. I wasn't sure I looked like Banya, but I certainly didn't look like Solene either. Nobody would mistake me for some well-dressed pet Lanati anymore.

Banya had a cloth sack with one strap that she always carried over her shoulder. I dumped out the contents, put back what I needed and pushed the rest under the bed. Then I added the scissors, the boot polish and brush, a flask of water and my embroidered pouch with the food-filled napkins, as well as most of the tea cakes wrapped in another napkin. I had to hope no one would stop me and inspect my sack. I would be hard-pressed to explain having fancy embroidered napkins from the Great Hall in my possession. I concealed the little pouch of money Monice had given me in my bodice or rather in the bodice of Banya's blouse, as that seemed the safest place at the moment.

Finally, I straightened out the tea things and hid away the

broken cups that had been the only real casualty. Then I went to the bed, kissed Banya on the forehead and whispered in her ear, "I'm so sorry for endangering your life this way." Much to my relief she was still breathing softly. I rolled her over toward the wall, brought the covers up around her, concealing her face, and spread some of my red hair on the pillow. What was left of it I slipped under the bed with the rest of my hidings.

There was now only one thing left to do. I went to the desk for a pen and paper and wrote, probably not very well since I had little practice at writing, a farewell note for Torvin.

My dearest Torvin, if you're reading this letter it means I'm already gone. I had to leave; if I stayed I would have died. Your brother said I was in need of taming. He was right, but taming would have killed me. I truly am a wild thing that needs its freedom, a creature of the forest. I cannot live in a cage no matter how beautiful, so I am running to save my life. Please don't try to come after me. If you bring me back I will surely die of grief or at my own hand, or by my actions I will force one of you to kill me. Please, I beg of you, believe what I say, for every word is true.

Torvin, I regret more than you can imagine the hurt I'm causing you. Know that I loved you, as much as any slave can love her master. And I believe you loved me too. I will always be grateful for your kindness and will think of you often.

I am escaping with no help but my own desperation. Banya and Dorial had no part in this and knew nothing of what I planned. I drugged Banya with the sleeping draught you gave me. I only hope that I didn't give her too much as I know nothing of such things. And I lied to Dorial, telling her I was sending Banya home to visit her sick grandmother, in order to masquerade as her myself.

Goodbye, Torvin, please think of me with love rather than hate or anger. I had no other choice. Understand, I need to be free or die in the attempt.

Your Friend Always,
Solene

My eyes darted around the room in a panic. I was not sure how to leave the note where Torvin would be sure to see it, but not see it any sooner than necessary. I almost tore it up. It seemed foolish to tell him everything, yet how else to spare Banya and Dorial some awful fate? But then how much could I trust the man anyhow, especially after I had betrayed him this way? I went back and forth, shifting from foot to foot, desperately needing to leave yet unable to resolve my dilemma. Suddenly I thought, what does it matter? If they find Banya unconscious in my bed, even before they find the note the game is already up and the gates closed against me. I left my message on the bed, hidden under Banya's hand.

I gave one last look around the room. Everything seemed in order. Dorial might think it strange that Banya wasn't removing the tea tray but that couldn't be helped. I couldn't risk a trip to the kitchen. Taking a deep breath to calm myself, I pulled Banya's kerchief low over my forehead to partially cover my darkened hair and tugged the collar of the blouse up around my cheeks. Then I turned the doorknob with a trembling hand.

When I opened the door Dorial sat up with a start. Apparently she had been dozing in her chair. She began shaking her head as if trying to clear it. "Is she asleep already?" she asked, her words slightly slurred.

I mumbled a quick "yes," trying to keep my face averted, glad the light in the hallway was dim, with only a few sconces spaced far apart and no windows to shine a bright light on my disguise.

"Are you off to your grandmother's then?" Her eyes were half-closed as if she was only keeping them open with great effort.

I nodded. Then I quickly handed her two little cakes from the tea, mumbling "for you" and "goodbye," and with another nod scurried past her down the hall, expecting at any moment to feel her hard hand gripping my arm.

She let me pass but called after me in an aggrieved tone, "You're very lucky to have a grandmother who lays claim to you, Banya. You should be grateful. I have no one at home who cares if I live or die." She sounded maudlin from drink. I *was* grateful, yes—but for the drink Dorial had consumed earlier. Had she been altogether sober I'm not sure I could have managed so easily.

When I passed the two guards at the end of the hall, I simply nodded to them in passing. Much to my relief they nodded back and didn't grab my arm and shout as I had half expected. I made my way to the kitchen stairs, keeping my head down and trying not to rush, even though everything in me wanted to run. It was lucky that Torvin had given me a thorough tour of the Palace or I wouldn't have known which way to go. Before I reached the bottom of the stairs I could hear the noise from the kitchen, the shouts and clang of pots, and see the steam billowing up. The smells made my stomach clench, reminding me how little I had eaten that day and how little I was likely to eat for a while.

I passed the entrance to the kitchen without anyone noticing me. They were far too busy, rushing to get the evening meal ready. When I put my hand on the latch for the outside door, I found I was shaking so badly I could hardly grasp it. I hesitated, afraid of what I might meet on the other side. Then I heard my mother's voice in my head saying, "I miss you, Solene, I want you home again." The words were as clear as if she had been standing right beside me. With that my hand steadied. I lifted the latch and stepped out into the Palace yard with Banya's little sack over my shoulder.

I was afraid that I would be met with an instant outcry, but no one paid the least attention to me. I might as well have been invisible. As I stepped out the door, four men came rushing in, carrying baskets and wooden boxes of produce for the kitchen. They would have knocked me down if I hadn't hastily moved aside. The bustle in the Palace courtyard had intensified with the afternoon's crowd, and no one stopped to take notice of one shabby servant.

Now there was just one last obstacle between me and freedom. I started for the stable, panicking as two carriages drove up to the grand stone archway of the front entrance and began to discharge passengers. I scurried into the stable entrance before any of them could turn my way, terrified someone would recognize me and just as frightened that someone who knew Banya would mistake me for her and try to talk to me.

It took a few moments for my eyes to adjust to the dimness inside, but I was grateful for it. All the better for the business I intended that there be many shadows and dark corners. Catching my breath, I stood very still, my back pressed against the wall, looking about and hoping to make some sense of my surroundings.

There was a great rush and bustle here as well as in the kitchen, with many horses being brought in and others out, men shouting and the constant rumble of wagons and carriages. I shivered. The place was cold even on this hot summer day and large enough that our big barn would have fit in it three times over. Finally I found the courage to move, hugging the stone wall to make sure I wouldn't get in the way of all this activity and so bring dangerous attention to myself.

Before long I came to a place where a long stout board with many clothes pegs mounted on it had been embedded in the wall. Most of the clothes it held were old tattered ones, work clothes probably left by their owners as they put on better ones for the festival. I found a battered cap, large enough to come down over my forehead, cover my ears and conceal a good part of my face, also an old shirt, which I slipped on over Banya's blouse, and trousers that were wide enough to cover Banya's bunched up skirt. All of this added considerably to my bulk and helped to conceal my identity. I took most of the coins from the little pouch between my breasts and slipped them into the pocket of my newly acquired pants. If I should need money on my way out of the city it wouldn't do to be groping in my shirt for it. Now I was feeling more confident, ready to go and find my horse.

That part, at least, was easily enough done. The horse was just where Monice had told me it would be, already saddled and bridled. I walked by the stall several times, only glancing at the horse in passing, trying to see if anyone was lying in wait there for me. It was hard to imagine that Monice was really going to help me escape. Now would be the perfect time and the best possible place for a trap. Ah well, *dead or gone by day's end, free either way*. Best get on with it. With the hair rising on the back of my neck, I went into the stall, walked up to the horse and stroked her forehead, realizing that I didn't even know her name. Too late for that now.

I had always had a good rapport with horses, and this one would likely be no different. Turning to rub her head against my sleeve, she made me smile as I untied her reins. *Almost there*, I whispered to give myself the courage to keep moving. I was actually feeling hopeful when a large hand gripped my shoulder and a harsh gravelly voice said almost in my ear, "Who are you and what are you doing with this horse?" The man sounded drunk and the reek of liquor suddenly enveloped me.

I froze. I was so terrified at that instant that I had no voice at all, probably for the best. Had I spoken then I might have sounded the way I felt, like a frightened little girl. As it was my forced silence gave me a moment or two to think.

Since I made no answer the man shook me hard. "Well?" he growled impatiently.

I cleared my throat and said in the deepest voice I could muster, "Let me go! Now! You're hurting my shoulder. I've been sent by the young master to fetch this horse for his mother."

He released me, but I could feel his reluctance. I turned to look at him. He was a large man, very ugly, with a warty, bulbous red nose, and evidently quite drunk. He was not looking at me in a kindly way. "Where's Marco?"

After only a moment's hesitation, the lie came easily enough, "Broke his leg pig wrestling and they sent me in his place." The man was still looking hostile and suspicious, unconvinced. On sudden inspiration I reached in my pocket and brought out some coins. "They said I was to give you these to go enjoy the festival."

His ugly face was instantly transformed by a huge grin. "Take good care of her then," he said. With that he slapped me on the back so hard he almost sent me sprawling and turned to stagger away, one more person who would probably suffer for my lies. This city was training me all too well.

Once he had left and no one in all that bustle seemed to be paying any attention to me, I took my chance to disguise the horse. Leading her into the shadows, I brushed brown boot polish into the star on her forehead and the white sock on her leg. Then I traded her ornate new bridle for an old shabby one, pushing the new one under a pile of manure. I was afraid to try changing saddles, so I threw a dusty feed sack over Monice's fancy one to keep it hidden.

Still staying close to the wall, I led the horse toward the entrance to watch for my opportunity. There was a crowd of men milling about there, too many for me to feel safe trying to pass them. My stomach churned with anxiety as I waited. I was beginning to think I was trapped there when a wagon rolled in. It was loaded high with sacks that I took to be grain. A shout for help went up and most of the men blocking my way rushed off to unload. No doubt this was what they had been waiting for. Now it was my time to move.

Keeping in the shadows as much as possible, I slipped out of the stable. Afraid that Ramule or Peltron might see and recognize the horse, I kept the wagons and carriages between me and the Palace as I walked her out the gates of the courtyard and into the street, free at least for that moment. Then, taking a deep breath to gather my strength, I mounted my borrowed horse and settled myself into the saddle. Once I was on her back, feeling her solid, comfortable bulk between my legs, some of my fear abated.

I had to navigate the city quickly. Day was fading fast. It would soon be dusk and I needed to be out of Hernorium. I was afraid that Torvin might be tempted to come back for one last look at me before going to the ball, perhaps hoping that I had recovered after all and would be able to dance with him. Or that Banya would awaken suddenly. Or that Ramule would go looking for his mother's horse. Or, worst of all, that Monice would betray me. If any of those things happened a signal would be given, and the gates of the city would quickly be closed against me, trapping me inside.

I wound through the streets, always heading for the west side of the lake, always heading down. Hoping not to encounter anyone who knew me, especially Peltron, I tried to stay to smaller streets, but sometimes those streets ended suddenly in a knot of dilapidated houses or even headed back up the hill again. In the middle of one of those clusters of houses, though, I found a little market that was almost deserted and risked buying some fruit, a loaf of bread and a round of cheese to add to my stash for later. I also bought a paper twist of fruit and cheese pastries to eat right away. I knew it was dangerous, but I needed food and Monice's money in my pocket was burning to be used. Besides, none of these people looked as if they might betray me to the Magistrar. They hardly seemed to notice me, though the woman at the stand gave a startled look of surprise at the coin I handed her. In my shabby clothes I suppose I looked like one of them.

After several more futile attempts to keep to the back ways, I ventured out onto larger streets and saw some of the places I had passed with Torvin and Banya during the day. At each corner I came to, each side street I passed, I braced for a sudden shout, an attack, being surrounded by armed men such as I had seen marching in the street that day. At one moment I thought I saw Ramule off in the distance with some other young men. And at another moment I thought I saw Peltron's blue and black carriage dashing up the hill. I had to keep reassuring myself that no one would recognize me now even if I were standing right next to them, not in those clothes and with that cap pulled low over my face.

Finally I made my way to Lake Street, just as Monice had told me, and followed it to the iron gate at the far west side of the lake. It was also standing open. There were guards lounging around it, but they were in a jolly mood, probably drunk, laughing and joking with each other and paying scant attention to who was coming in or out, especially who was going out. Holding my breath in suspense, I kept moving forward until I had passed through the gate. Shivers were running up and down my back, but no voice shouted, no hand reached out, no one stopped me. I rode from cobbled streets out onto a broad paved road with nothing blocking my way. This had to be the Westway. I began to breath a little easier.

A short distance down the road I turned back for one last look at Hernorium. The city rose behind me, going steeply up the hill to the Palace compound, massive, complex, beautiful, a magnificent sight, its cruelty hidden by distance. The westering sun was flashing gold and red in the windows' glass, lighting the Palace with mock fire, giving it an eerie beauty. I thought I could see my window from there—not mine anymore, I quickly reminded myself. After a few more bends in the road I left the city behind and was moving out into the countryside.

I guided the horse over to the grassy verge and sent her into a trot. She was wonderfully responsive, and I fell into an easy rhythm with her. Since I didn't know her name I called her Mercy for saving me from Hernorium. I wanted to make a strong bond with her and have her become familiar with my hands and voice so I stroked her neck and talked to her constantly, saying whatever nonsense flowed through my head at that moment. Somewhere down the road my life might depend on her friendship. Besides, she was the only company I would have for a while. I fell silent when others passed. I didn't want to be noticeable in any way, certainly not to be remembered as the crazy girl talking to her horse as if it could really understand. People were still flowing into the city in large numbers, probably for the evening's festivities or going to dance at the ball, that ball where I would never dance with Torvin.

Gone! Not dead! Not dead! a voice in my head sang. *Free! Free!* I was riding into darkness, dressed in stolen clothes on a stolen/borrowed horse, possibly about to be lost on a strange road, probably with deadly pursuit soon to be following, yet at that moment I felt no fear, only a wild elation. I wanted to sing, to shout, to howl like a wolf. Joy bubbled up in my blood like strong wine. "I'm not dead," I said to the little horse, trotting along steadily under me. "I'm free, gone from the city, heading home." I think I had never in my life felt so conscious of being happy.

* * *

As soon as I could, I left the main road that was still crowded with people coming and going from the festival and found myself a little side road that skirted the fields and wound through the woods. With the horse going at a steady trot I kept moving through the late afternoon and well into the night, wanting to put as much distance as possible between me and the city and those men. At first I kept smiling, even humming to myself, savoring the feelings of freedom, the things I had always taken for granted before my capture: the warmth of the sun on my shoulders, the light breeze in my face, the sound of birds singing, the rhythm of the horse's hooves moving under me. Then, gradually, as darkness came on, the elation of escape began to wear off. Fear came in its place as the reality of my situation set in and I thought of what lay ahead.

Before being taken captive I'd lived all my life in a world of safety. The furthest I'd ever gone from home had been to the neighboring settlement of Hamlin with my mother and sister and once to the town of Melvais with some of the other girls, riding there together, spending the night with friends and coming back the next day. Even if I was gone all day in my wanderings, I always came back at night for shelter and companionship and food. In my whole life I'd never spent a night alone in the woods. Now the ever deepening darkness seemed to be full of strange sounds that in the daytime might just have been the little noises of the forest talking to itself. At night these same sounds became sinister and threatening, ominous rustlings, slitherings, growls and hisses. The crunching of leaves and the snapping of twigs coming from unseen sources, close by me but invisible, made the hair prickle on the back of my neck. There was just enough moonlight to be able to see a little, but under the trees the moving light and shadows shifted into frightening patterns. Brushing suddenly against leaves or twigs sent shivers of apprehension up my back. Several times I had to bite back a cry of fear at their ghostly touch. Even the horse seemed nervous, trotting faster and tossing her head from side to side as if she might bolt at any moment. I kept talking to her, trying to calm her and also to give myself courage.

After a while Mercy began to stumble. I myself had grown so tired I found I was swaying in the saddle, but I dreaded stopping. Being on the horse's back seemed like some sort of protection. Having my feet on the ground would put me where something, anything, could get at me. Finally I had no choice. Otherwise I might have toppled off, which would have been far worse.

I tied the horse to a tree. Deciding to use the feedbag as a sort of crude bed, I groped around in the semi-darkness for enough leaves to stuff it with. In that way I made a place for myself on the rough hard ground. Next I pulled off Banya's bunched up skirt, glad to finally be free of it, and rolled it up for a pillow. I had no light as I worked. The candle I brought had a wick that seemed impervious to fire, and the matches kept going out in my shaky hand. Finally I gave up and curled up on my noisily rustling bed of leaves, frightened as I had never been before in my life, too frightened even to cry. I wrapped my arms around myself for comfort, sure there was no way I could fall asleep, not all alone there in that awful place, with the sounds of the night so close around me. But weary as I was, sleep took me down in minutes.

I woke in a panic and leapt to my feet, wanting to run and unable to decide which way to go since the terrifying sounds seemed to be coming from all directions. As I stood there, staring into the moonlight-dappled darkness, caught between fear and indecision, my mind gradually cleared of sleep and I realized I was surrounded by nothing more than owls having one of their raucous nighttime conversations with each other. Sounds that at home thrilled us when we were sitting up around a late-night fire, here, alone in the woods, had provoked terror. Feeling foolish, I lay down again on my bed of leaves. This time I wrapped my arms around myself for warmth as well as comfort since the night had grown quite chilly. I slept fitfully and was glad to be up and moving as soon as there was some faint gray light.

I began taking smaller and smaller roads, hoping to stay away from people and so avoid pursuit. Monice had said to keep the sun at my back in the morning and in my face in the afternoon. I tried but sometimes there was no sun, and sometimes the woods were too thick, and sometimes the road did not run straight but seemed to twist around and turn back on itself. At home I was never lost in the woods. No matter how far I strayed I always found my way back. There I knew every road and path, and I had a good sense of how the land lay so I could find my way even without a path. Here I was a stranger and the woods were not my friend. I was afraid to ask anyone for directions for fear that would mark me as an outsider and so lead to questions and perhaps betrayal if Peltron's men came this way. I was even afraid of letting the horse graze too long for fear of the attention it might bring. Never in my life had I felt so lonely. And it was not just pursuit I feared, it was hunger as well. My food was quickly running out.

That first day I had eaten everything I took from the Palace wrapped in a napkin. It was all strange-looking and crushed together, almost unrecognizable, but it tasted unbelievably good. Though I was very hungry I tried to make it last. For the next few days I rationed out the bread and cheese, though by the end of it the bread was so hard I had to soak it in water and the cheese had little green spots that I scraped off with my fingernail. Had I been in the woods of home I could have found edible roots and leaves, but I would still have needed a pot and a fire to cook them. Here all my knowledge of the woods did me little good. I found some berries that I quickly gobbled down, and some wild summer lettuce that was almost too bitter from lack of rain to be edible. I also picked up a few pieces of unfamiliar fruit that had fallen from the trees. The first of them instantly puckered my mouth when I bit into it, so I quickly threw the rest away.

I kept moving, but I was no longer sure which way to go. In losing pursuit I had also lost myself. In just a few days I had gone from feeling elated at my escape and pleased with my cleverness to being lost and hungry and frightened. It was as if I had used up my whole store of courage, spirit and ingenuity just escaping the city.

Adana had talked with such enthusiasm about adventure. Well, she could have it! It was not for me. In this past month I'd had enough to last the rest of my life. Here I was, caught against my will in an adventure not of my choosing, and I wanted nothing more than to be home again, safe in my own bed. Adana had accused me of being my mother's baby and maybe she was right. At that moment it was my mother, Elani, I longed for far more than Adana. Indeed I found myself crying for her at night, longing for the touch of her hand or the sound of her gentle voice that I feared I would never hear again.

I had eaten nothing for a long while, had lost track of time and was riding along, dejected and weary, frightened of everything, sure I was lost, not knowing which way to turn or what to do next. I had been out at least five days. This was early on the morning of the sixth day or perhaps it was the seventh or maybe even the eighth. The sky was a solid gray so there was no sunlight or shadow to help guide me. I was well past urging the horse to trot. In fact I was just letting her plod along at her own pace, sometimes stopping to graze at the side of the road and sometimes even choosing the way when there was a choice to be made. It hardly seemed to matter anymore.

I finally came to the end of the small road I had been traveling and met with a wider and much more traveled one. The horse stopped in the middle of it, this time waiting for a signal from me, but I had no idea which way to turn. Feeling stupid and helpless, I sat for a long time, looking first in one direction and then the other. It hardly seemed worth the effort to go on. I had neither the will nor the strength to continue this struggle to stay alive. I was just thinking it might be best to free the horse and lie down in the leaves to wait for sleep or death—whichever claimed me first—when I heard a wagon coming. I knew I should get off the road and hide. Instead I just sat there, staring in the direction of the sound and waiting for my fate. Long before I could see anything I heard the clop of hooves and the creak of wagon wheels, then the sound of a woman's voice, singing loudly and joyfully.

As if caught in a spell, I watched her approaching—an amazing sight. The wagon had a curved top that arched high over her head. It was covered with a patchwork of brightly patterned material, all decorated and edged with ribbons and tassels that fluttered in the wind, along with bells that made a constant shimmering music—a moving fantasy, outlandish and wonderful. The sides of the wagon, as well as the wagon's wheels, were painted in intricate designs. The woman herself was dressed in colors as bold as the wagon top. A little dog sat up on the seat beside her, coat red as a fox. The woman had her head thrown back, singing with abandon. Hungry and weary as I was, I resented her good fortune. So much gaiety seemed like an affront to me, an insult. She, no doubt, had food in her wagon, as much as she wanted, and a dry bed every night. She knew where she was going, and clearly no one was in pursuit, trying to kill her.

Only a few feet away she drew her wagon to a halt. We sat staring at each other for a long moment while her little dog yipped wildly. I was longing to speak to her, yet I dared not ask for her help. I was just about to turn my horse back into the relative safety of the woods when she asked in a tone of amazement, "Are you really Solene? Is it possible that I've actually found you?"

I shook my head wildly. "No! No! My name is Magya!" Now I was ready to set the horse into a gallop and disappear down the road.

She laughed, a lovely musical sound. "No use lying to me girl. I saw you on Torvin's arm the day of the festival. It's just that you look so changed it took me a moment or two to recognize you. What a stroke of luck. The fact is I've been hoping to find you. No point running. You're quite safe with me. Think about it, I'm no threat to you. I'm in a slow-moving wagon and you're on a horse that can go a great deal faster."

I looked at her warily, still prepared to flee, watching the back of the wagon in case it contained armed men who would suddenly spring out at me.

"How did you catch up with me?"

"Good question. I didn't really expect to. I left the next morning so you must have lost at least a day and half, circling around and getting lost on unfamiliar roads. It's only traveler's luck that we crossed paths, that and some good guesses and my long knowledge of these roads."

"Traveler's luck," I said bitterly. "That certainly wasn't with me the day I was captured." There was something warmly seductive about her voice and her little dog and her cozy-looking wagon. It would be so pleasant to sink down in the seat beside her and maybe be offered something to eat. The smells of food were wafting up from the wagon, and I found myself leaning toward it. With a groan I straightened my back, struggling to stay alert. "How do I know I can trust you?"

With that she gave a snort of annoyance. "Great Mother! Is there no end to her questions? How this and how that! How indeed! Do I look like someone who would carry tales for the Magistrar?" She leaned forward to glare at me. Then her expression suddenly changed. In the next instant she threw her head back and laughed, making all the little bells on her scarf and in her hair jingle gaily.

I thought she was mocking me and a flush of anger burned up my face. "How would I know?" I asked sharply. "What do I know of that city? I was a prisoner there. The only people I was allowed to talk to were my two maids and Torvin. The only time I ever saw the city was the day of the festival. What sort of a festival is that anyway, where they train dogs to rip each other to pieces and men are lashed with whips to make them row faster? We have festivals at home and they're nothing like that."

She shook her head and answered more seriously. "I wasn't mocking you, only laughing at the thought that I could be working for the Magistrar. Not likely. I must tell you, Solene, there are many decent people in that city and a whole other life there not easily seen from inside the Palace walls. But of course, with the terrible way you were brought there, you could hardly be expected to know that. Yes, you can trust me. Actually I've been hoping to find you. I needed to warn you that Peltron is planning to come after you with a whole troop of his men. He thinks to raid your settlement as well and take back all the women there or at least the ones that are young and useful. The others..." She shrugged and went on quickly, "He intends to parade his captives up and down Grand Avenue for everyone to see before they are given to his men as Lanati. Torvin is trying to talk him out of it. He says to let you be, but Peltron is determined to teach you a lesson, make an example of you in front of the whole city."

"A lesson? What sort of lesson?" These people were incomprehensible to me.

"The lesson that a Lanati cannot defy the will of the Magistrar. A Lanati is property and supposed to have no will of her own. I must tell you, Solene, the whole city is abuzz with your escape. Most of the common folk are delighted with it. There are all sorts of stories flying about, each more amazing than the last. I can assure you that Peltron and his father are not pleased. They have been made to look like fools in front of everyone. Peltron swears he will have you back, alive or dead."

I shook my head in bewilderment. "But I wasn't trying to defy anyone. I only needed to be free or I would have died there."

"Ah, but a Lanati's life is not her own to do with as she pleases, and it usually doesn't last very long. You did well to be away from there. Of all people, I understand only too well the need to be free. You at least don't mind living in a settlement, while I cannot even abide being in one place for more than a few days at a time. Then my feet get itchy and I have to move on."

I stared at her, captured by her fierce energy and her rapid flow of words. "What drives you to go on that way?"

"Oh, I've been like that for years. I grew up in a house where my father and brother abused me. By the time I was fourteen I decided I had a choice; I could kill them both or I could leave. I would have been glad enough to kill them and had already sharpened the knife, but I had a mother I loved and for some reason she loved those men. I couldn't do that to her, so instead I left with the family horse and wagon, thinking they owed me something after all that. I gave my brother a good slash across his arm when he tried to stop me and I've been traveling ever since." Her words came tumbling out so fast I could hardly follow them.

When there was a pause I asked, "Have you ever been back?"

"Yes, to see my mother, but with a big knife on my belt. No one thinks to bother me now. But enough of such pleasant talk. Precious time is passing and there's little to spare. Tie your horse to the back of the wagon and get in. We can talk on the way. You must be tired and thirsty and hungry and are no doubt lost."

With a sigh I surrendered to fate and did as she told me, tying my horse in back and climbing with some difficulty up on the seat beside her. I was either fatally doomed or incredibly lucky. By now I was too tired to care. It felt good just to lean back against soft cushions. This woman had made a cozy little nest of her wagon with mats and rugs and cushions and baskets, all in bright colors and all slightly worn and shabby.

"It's just as you say. I'm all of those things," I told her with another deep sigh. "My food is all gone and so is my water, and in truth I don't know the way home any more. In making sure they couldn't find me I've lost myself in these woods. I feel as if I've been going in circles." At that moment I was so weary I was close to tears.

"There's a jug of water by your feet and a basket of food under this bench. Help yourself to both, but leave a little for me. You're not too terribly lost, but we have a ways to go yet and probably won't be there till evening. My name is Josian the Wagoner, and we have a good deal to talk of as we travel. I've never been to your settlement, though I'm thinking I might like to add it to my trading route. I'll keep going in that direction, and when the way begins to look familiar to you then you can guide me in."

I was grateful for food and water, but I was not to get any sleep for awhile, as she kept asking me a string of questions about my life and my capture and especially my escape, which story I had to tell her several times over. After a while food and drink somewhat revived me. "Did they chase after me?" I asked when I could get in a question of my own.

"Yes, but not until the next morning. You must have had a good start on them by then. I was at the fish market just below the Palace when they set out. There was a big commotion, much shouting back and forth and galloping up and down. They came back quickly enough when they couldn't find you right away. Peltron wanted to assemble a more organized pursuit. That was when they decided to raid the settlement instead of just bringing back one woman and for that they needed to make real preparations. We must go warn your people to get ready for a raid, though what they can do against such a force is hard to imagine. Perhaps they can just flee and so hope to save their lives. I think Peltron will be merciless. He's very angry, not used to being crossed in that way. No one ever opposes Peltron except his brother, Torvin, who is a very different sort of man and who, for some reason, he loves."

"But Peltron doesn't even know the way to Nessian. He only found me by accident."

"He knows. He's talked to traders who have been there."

"And they told him? I thought they were our friends."

"He persuaded them to talk. He can be very persuasive."

I didn't want to think too much about his methods or what might have happened to our friends. "How do you know so much about that city?"

"I trade there often and talk to everyone and so have a web of friends who give me information, some even within the Palace itself. Servants hear everything and no one notices them. The masters think of them as moving furniture, useful and mindless, but they know everything that goes on. They're always watching and quite willing to talk to someone like me since I bring them little things from other places."

Now it was time for the questions I'd been dreading. "What of Banya? What of Dorial? Were they blamed for my escape?

Were they tortured? Killed?"

Josian shook her head. "The truth of it is I know Dorial from years back. She was a friend from my village. She left at almost the same time I did and for much the same reason. She told me Peltron would have had them killed and no doubt tortured first, but Torvin would not allow it. He found your note and protected them. Banya was still drugged the next morning. They had a hard time bringing her around. You must have given her quite a dose. I think both of them will just be sent back to work in the kitchen. That stableman was not so lucky. He was found asleep at a tavern table. He kept saying someone had given him a handful of coins to go enjoy the festival. As I was leaving the city I heard Peltron was planning to have him hanged for neglecting his duty."

I shivered, thinking of the man with the red nose and the big grin going off so happily to his fate with my coins in his hand. "And now what's going to happen?" My relief at being rescued abruptly turned to despair at the thought of bringing home death—or at least having it follow me there. And guilt too, as if somehow this was all my fault. If only I had stayed in the city and accepted my fate the women of my settlement would have been spared. Too late now, the soup was in the pot. "What are we going to do, Josian? They will destroy us. I've seen those men with their armor and their weapons marching down the avenue at festival. They're terrifying. There's no way we can stand against such a force. No one could. And we have no weapons. We're not fighters. We're farmers and potters and weavers, not warriors."

She nodded, looking thoughtful. Then she smiled, a sly little fox-like smile. "There are always ways—if one is clever enough. If you can't win with weapons then you must use your wits instead. I think we have a week or two, probably more to get ready. Now that they're making a project of it and not just chasing down one unarmed woman, it will take them a while to prepare properly."

"Are you planning to stay and help us?" That gave me a little hope.

"Me? Why not? Living as I do my time is my own. You might need my experience. Besides, I wouldn't want to miss it." To my amazement she was actually grinning with pleasure.

"But there's no way..."

"Enough now. I have some ideas cooking. Sleep for a while and let me think. I'll wake you if I believe we're close to your settlement. At any rate, we won't be there till much later in the day."

Now I wanted to urge her to hurry, to go faster, to run the horse. "But how can we...?"

"Sleep! Now!" she ordered. "We'll talk later."

I nodded. An interesting person, my rescuer—disturbing also. On the surface she had the lighthearted gaiety of the road traveler. Under that I could feel the iron that held her together. I had no doubt she could have killed those abusive men. Feeling I had not much choice, I slumped down sideways in the seat. The little dog curled up next to me, my good friend now that I had given her some scraps. I was sure I couldn't sleep, was much too worried, had too much on my mind. But I was also very tired, exhausted actually. The wagon was like a giant cradle rocking me as it went, and Josian began singing again, softly this time, like a lullaby.

Later, just at dusk, Josian shook me awake. "I know you couldn't sleep, Solene, but you've been snoring like a saw trying to cut through wet wood. Time to wake up. I have a feeling we're close."

Instantly I sat bolt upright and looked around. Familiar road ahead of us, familiar woods on one side and familiar fields on the other. "Yes!" I shouted. "Yes, yes, yes! Just go a little farther on this road, then turn left between two huge old trees, follow that way a few more miles and take the right fork. We're almost there."

After a while Josian began to sing a weaving song I knew. I joined her in the chorus, though she had a much better voice and seemed to know all the words. As we passed familiar places, joy and fear were warring in my heart. I was so glad to be home and so afraid of what was to come, dreading sharing my news with the women of Nessian. We had only sung four verses before we swept around the corner and there it all was in front of me, the familiar houses and streets and gardens of home. Tears stung my eyes.

Several women, drawn by curiosity, rushed out at our approach as we trotted noisily up the cobbled main street of our little settlement. Some of my aunts and cousins were among them and they began shouting my name excitedly when I called out to them. My mother was standing in her doorway, looking puzzled. With a yell I jumped out of the wagon before it had fully stopped and ran past everyone else. Shouting and sobbing, I threw my arms around her and she covered my face with kisses while our tears ran together. In my ear she kept saying, over and over, "Oh, Solene, I thought you were lost to us. I'm so glad to see you back! So glad! So glad!"

Finally I pulled away a little. "I escaped, but the story isn't over yet, Elani. There's worse coming, much worse."

She shook her head vehemently. "What could be worse than losing you?"

"Much worse," I said urgently. "Much much worse. We have to get ready for it and quickly."

By then women from all over the settlement were shouting my name, running up and surrounding us. Adana pushed her way through to give me a huge hug. "I was so afraid for you and so sorry for everything I said in anger. Please forgive me, Solene. Welcome home and know that I love you." Then she held me away a little to look at my face. By now my scarf had slipped off my head and settled around my neck. "But what on earth have you done with your hair? I would hardly know you."

"Scissors and boot polish," I told her with a laugh. "It was to help me stay safe. Red hair is much too visible and obvious."

Then my sister Karil appeared behind my mother. She had that mingled look of admiration and resentment I so often saw on her face when she looked at me. She hugged me too, but I sensed some resistance there, as if she was not altogether glad to see me home, as if perhaps she thought her life would have been better if I had stayed away.

61

When I looked back, Josian was slowly getting out of her wagon, holding her little dog in her arms, waiting for the commotion to die down. "And here is the woman who rescued me and brought me home," I called out, making a wide gesture toward her with my arm.

She laughed her tinkling laugh, made a mock bow and held up a hand. "Not so, I didn't rescue Solene. She rescued herself, very bravely and cleverly I must say. I just gave her a ride back home."

Now Josian was surrounded with eager thanks, an assault of questions and many offers of food. Meanwhile I ducked into my mother's house to find some warm water and wash the greasy mess out of my hair. I came back out feeling pounds lighter and more like my old self. Afterward, though the hour was late, we all gathered at the meeting place in front of Headwoman Namuri's house. Food was brought from everywhere, also chairs, benches and cushions as we quickly assembled for an informal meeting.

After I had related my story one more time, Namuri told me that Valdru and Tarsel and Senli had been captured the same day that I had been. My heart sank. I feared for all of them, but especially for Valdru who was my cousin and my closest friend from childhood on. Picturing all the terrible things that could have happened to them, I felt sick with grief. I was free and they were captives in that city.

"I saw it all," Huldra said. "We were riding home through the woods, coming back from visiting Nadir at the settlement of Hamlin. I was mounted on the back of Tarsel's horse because mine was lame that day. I had slipped off and stepped behind some bushes to relieve myself when those men came riding up the path. They snatched the other three and I could do nothing but watch. No way could I have stopped them. If I had made any move they just would have had me too. They didn't think to look for me since there were only three horses. I was trembling inside, but I made myself stay very still for fear the slightest motion would betray my presence. After they rode off, I ran back to tell everyone here what had happened."

Elani shook her head and said to me, "We thought they must have taken you too since you disappeared at the same time. We went later and found a mass of hoof prints and also footprints, as well as your mushroom bag. I thought I'd never see you again." She began crying and hugging me again. I wanted to tell her to stop. I could see my sister glaring at me across the circle.

Soon the mothers and sisters and grandmothers and cousins of the missing women were bombarding me with questions. "Have you seen them? Are they all right? What have those men done with them? Will they be able to escape too? Will they be home soon?"

To all their questions I had to keep answering, "I don't know. I haven't seen them. I didn't even know who was taken. I was never out of the Palace until the day of the festival, the day I myself escaped." One question I could have answered and chose not to was their chances of escape. I was afraid they were much reduced by my disappearance. Unfortunately, because of me, those women would probably be that much better guarded.

After that Josian told everything she knew of the impending raid and in turn was bombarded with questions. For a while there was much excited talk. Finally, speaking loud enough to be heard over all the other voices, Namuri said, "We have had our little problems here, but we have never faced anything like this." At that everyone fell silent. Namuri went on, speaking to Josian, "You live in the world out there and better know their ways. What do you suggest we do?"

All eyes turned on Josian. For a moment it looked as if her confidence wavered. Then she sucked in her breath, nodded and began speaking with slow dignity. "A heavy question to entrust to one Woman Wagoner and a stranger at that, but I'll do my best. That's all I thought about while Solene slept on our way here. First of all, you must understand, you cannot meet these men in armed combat. Solene has seen them, she will tell you the same thing. They would mow you down in a bloody heap or capture you easily enough if that was their intent. Nothing will be gained and everything lost by trying to meet them in battle. It must all

63

be done by trickery and cleverness. No use to have a bunch of farmers out on the field of battle, fighting off armed men with their pitchforks. Tragic folly, you can never win that way. You'll only end up fertilizing your fields with your own blood.

"Now this is the hard thing to say. I would advise you to abandon your settlement. Some of you take your children, your animals, your food goods and anything else you value and go into hiding. Move everything out of harm's way. They may destroy your buildings, but at least they won't kill your people and your livestock. Some of you stay here, hidden, to keep watch. The rest of you, the youngest and strongest, I will teach you how to wield swords to defend yourselves. First we will have to make some. You should also enlist the help of other young women in the neighboring settlements. If men from Hernorium continue marauding here, they too are at risk. With this trained troop of ours we must lure Peltron into a trap and use Solene as the bait since she is the one he really wants."

When she finished speaking there was such an explosion of loud protests and arguments no woman could hear another. My mother grabbed my arm, shouting, "Not Solene, I won't allow it. I already lost her once. I won't let it happen again!"

I shook off her hand and said sharply, "Mine to decide, Elani."

Finally Namuri banged loudly on a pot and shouted for silence. Gradually some calm was restored and we began to discus Josian's ideas in a more orderly way, still mostly by objecting to them. The thought of abandoning our settlement was abhorrent to us and the thought of using one of our own for bait was unthinkable. At last, after much talk without much clarity, Namuri said wearily, "I understand that Josian's ideas are not very appealing. Neither is a deadly raid from the city of Hernorium, a raid over which we have no control and about which we have no choice. If anyone has a better idea, let her put it forward now."

At that there was total silence. We all looked at each other expectantly, hoping for answers, but no one spoke. After a while of tense silence Namuri went on, "Well, I think we have our answer clearly enough. It's late. I suggest we go home and sleep on all this and meet again here at the first light of morning to plan our actions and divide the work."

Afterward Adana came and took my arm. "Come sleep with me, Solene." I nodded in numb silence. With my head against her shoulder and her arm around my waist we walked into the house together, our small quarrels forgotten for the moment in our much larger troubles.

I spent much of that night sobbing in Adana's arms, weeping from relief, from anger, from grief, while she tried her best to comfort me. She held me close, stroked my hair, whispered soothing words in my ear, but no matter how much she loved me or I loved her, nothing she did could touch that bottomless pit of sorrow. "It will be all right, Love," she murmured to me. "We have each other again. You'll see, it will pass, things will come right again."

I clung to her, wanting to believe her words, wanting them to be true. But I knew deep inside that things were changed forever. They would never come right again. I had grown up an innocent. I had left our house that fateful morning an innocent. And then I had met with a swift, violent education and had seen a whole other side of human beings. I had never known people could be so brutal to each other, so cruel. Now there was no way I could forget everything I knew or unlearn everything I had seen and felt. It was lodged in my body as well as in my mind. In time perhaps I would live it down, but I would never again be the same girl who had walked out into the woods that day.

Later, while Adana slept, I lay there feeling the wonderful soft warmth of her body against mine, listening with pleasure to her gentle breathing and puzzling over my tangled relationship with my sister Karil and our mother Elani. Karil used to say to me, "She loves you more than me because you were really the child of her body. I was just one of those cast-off unwanted girl-babies that men bring here and we take in. She didn't want the bother of another pregnancy and she thought you shouldn't grow up alone, so she got me to keep you company, like a big doll." I knew this wasn't true. I knew Elani adored Karil and grieved over her unhappiness. When Karil would start in that way I always wanted to say something cruel like, "Well, she shouldn't have bothered," or "I might have been better off alone," but Elani would tell me, "Be kind, Solene, you're the oldest. She's unhappy, don't make it worse."

I always thought Marn, our other mother, left because of Grandmother Orlin's meanness and I know it had hurt Karil even more than me. "Marn was my real mother," Karil would say. "She really loved me." Sometimes she would blame me for Marn's departure, but in truth Marn abandoned us all, leaving suddenly and without a word. We heard later from some traders that she had gone to live in a city on "the Outside." Elani was devastated. I think she always hoped Marn would come back after Orlin died of snakebite, but by then Marn must have made a life elsewhere that didn't include us. She never came back and we had had no word from her. We weren't even sure if she was still alive, but Elani had gotten into the habit of waiting. I think that was why she never took another companion though I know for certain there had been several offers. I often wondered if Karil would have been a different person if Marn had stayed, more trusting, less jealous and unhappy.

The next morning dawned all too soon. I had hardly slept. I woke groggily, wondering for a moment where I was and how I had gotten there. In the next instant I was flooded with joy at finally being home, quickly followed by worry over what was to come. In spite of my lack of sleep, I leapt up with a great sense of urgency. Along with Adana I dashed off to the meeting place, with Elani and Karil rushing to keep up with us. Others were speedily gathering from all sides, carrying pots of food, loaves of bread and wheels of cheese.

When we got there the circle was already humming with agitated talk. It took some effort for Namuri to bring us all to silence, rapping on the ground with her cane. She asked who needed to speak. Almost immediately Karil jumped up to claim the center of attention. "I think it's cowardly to back down before these men, to let them drive us out of our own village and destroy everything we've built without a fight. We should have some honor. Surely if Josian can teach us how to use swords we can find a way to defend what is ours." At once several of the other young women joined in, talking excitedly about arming ourselves and fighting back. To my dismay Adana was among them, echoing Karil's words, saying "I don't want these men to think women are so easily frightened and can't protect themselves." Then Karil jumped in again, "I am ready to train with Josian, but only if I can help make a line of defense in front of our village. I, for one, don't plan on running away."

I felt a mounting irritation with my sister, trying to make herself sound bold and brave when she knew nothing of the realities we faced. At last I jumped in, also on my feet, "Don't be a fool, Karil! You're just talking that way to make yourself seem large. You have no idea what these men are like. I've seen them, I know."

Instantly she shot back, "Just because you've been to the city doesn't mean you know everything and can tell the rest of us what to do."

I was outraged. "What do you mean 'been to the city'? Do you think I went there for pleasure? For entertainment? Don't you remember? I was captured, taken against my will and used." At the end of this I was yelling and there were tears in my eyes.

"Enough, both of you," Namuri said forcefully, pointing her cane at each of us in turn. "This is not the time to sort out sisterly quarrels. There are more important things at stake here."

Seeing the look of distress on my mother's face I sat down again and fell silent. I was hurt and angry, stung by the unfairness of Namuri's words. Josian stood up in my place. She swept us all with her eyes and then settled on Karil. "I'm not your enemy, Karil. I've seen the enemy and trust me, they don't look anything like me. They're hard and strong, armed and trained. They wear heavy chain-and-leather armor that's difficult to pierce and they march or ride together in formation. There is nothing honorable about standing in front of a death machine and getting yourself mowed down. If we want to survive this onslaught and come out alive and even win, then we will have to use our wits in dishonorable and clever ways, all of us putting our heads together on it." It both amazed and touched me to hear Josian say "our" and "we" as if she were truly one of us.

Next she turned to Adana. "You say you don't want to seem frightened. You'd be wise to be very frightened. I witnessed such a raid once, not from Hernorium but from the city of Kalthar. I only survived because I was hidden, along with a few others. The Magistrar of that city wanted a certain valley for pasturing his cattle. There was already a little village there blocking his way. The people were told to leave, though there had been a settlement there for almost two hundred years. When they refused, he sent his men to clear them out.

"The people of the village, armed with their pitchforks and their knives, went out boldly to confront the raiders, shouting at them to leave immediately. They were very brave and very foolish. Soon they were very dead, quickly ridden down and slaughtered where they stood in a spreading river of blood. At the end not one of them was left alive. When the raiders finished with the people they herded away the animals. The cowards, or perhaps the wise ones, were the ones hiding up in the rocks with me. We were the only ones left alive, too few of us even to bury the dead. I don't propose we surrender. I propose we find a way to win that won't cost us all our lives."

Josian's words or perhaps her graphic picture silenced our objections, and there was no more talk of honor or courage or of mounting a line of defense in front of those men. The rest of the meeting was spent raising ideas and formulating plans. At the end of it Namuri got to her feet with great difficulty, leaning heavily on her cane. Shaking her head, she said wearily, "We have lived quietly and peacefully here for all these years. I never expected to face such choices in my lifetime, but these are new times. If one group of men can breach the old agreements, then how many others will come after them?"

Looking at her I thought how much Namuri had aged since

this began. In truth, she was not much older than my mother, but she looked to be of another generation. I saw how the lines had deepened around her eyes and mouth. She was hunched forward, her shoulders rounded as if with weight, as if almost overnight the work of keeping Nessian safe had become a crushing burden instead of a round of well-loved familiar chores. Even her lameness appeared more pronounced. Namuri was a capable Headwoman. For as long as I could remember she had run our settlement with firmness, kindness and skill, but this violent incursion into our lives might be too much for her. After all, nothing like this had ever happened before. I wondered if she might step down when it was over.

After the meeting I was questioned further by the mothers of the missing girls, led by my aunt Lucian, Valdru's mother, a very persistent questioner who thought I might still have some useful piece of information hidden away in a recess of my brain. Though I called her "aunt" out of respect, she was actually my mother's older cousin. My mother had no sisters. Grandmother Orlin had said many times, "One child was nuisance enough. I can't imagine being fool enough to saddle myself with another," though I couldn't think Elani was anything but a quiet compliant loving child, hardly a nuisance. It was Lucian who had remained my mother's friend after Orlin had driven everyone else away from our door with her meanness. And it was Lucian who became our second second-mother when Marn left suddenly and Elani was so devastated she could hardly get out of bed, much less care for two children and a house. Lucian took care of us and kept the house together until my mother recovered enough to take charge. Then she helped my mother again when Orlin died.

I loved Lucian, she was a wonderful woman, but I would never want to be on her wrong side. It would be like getting in front of a moving wagon. In Nessian we often joked about her being our second Headwoman because she was so quick to take charge in any situation. Much as she loved me, I think she resented that I was home and free while her daughter was trapped in that city. Over and over she asked, "Are you sure you never heard her name mentioned or caught a glimpse of her?" until I finally lost my temper and shouted, "I was a prisoner there in a room ten stories above the street. How was I to see anyone?"

She took a step back. "Well, you don't have to be rude and yell at me. Surely you can understand how worried I am." I told her I was sorry and we hugged, both of us in tears. Finally I was allowed to go.

Walking home from the meeting, I was suddenly struck by the beauty of this place where I had lived all my life. My great-great-great-grandmothers had chosen well. Nessian lay in a small fertile valley, shaped like a long bowl and circled by hills. The river that was the source of our water and the place for our summer bathing ran along one edge and across the bottom of the valley. We were surrounded by woods, well out of the way of any large roads—Peltron and his men had found us by accident—but close enough to the settlement of Hamlin and Balsheer for easy contact and even close enough to the town of Tremorn for the pregnancy procedure that granted us our babies. Our two hundred or so houses spilled across the narrow end of the valley with paths and roads winding between them. Pastures, gardens and orchards ran down the length of the valley to the river.

I stopped and stared around me, seeing it all with new eyes, as if I hadn't grown up here, as if I were really seeing it for the very first time, something incredibly beautiful and precious that was about to be destroyed. Years and years of women's work. Not perfect, of course. I could wander through and find a gate or shutter hanging loose, some rocks fallen from a wall, a shed roof in need of repair. And yet all perfect: lush flower gardens spilling out into the pathways; the carefully built stone walls of our houses that had stood for years against all weather, thatch gleaming in the sunlight; fruit trees heavy with summer fruit; carved benches for sitting and talking with friends and neighbors. It was all simple and ordinary and yet all unbelievably, gloriously beautiful in the noonday sun, my great-great-great-grandmothers' dream come true. Ducks passed by me, marching together from one pond to another and I started to laugh. I spotted a small orange and white kitten playing in a shaft of sunlight and suddenly found myself in tears, leaning against a tree, weeping and afraid, seeing it all in ruins.

Those next few weeks I think we all worked harder than ever before in our lives, moving and securing everything we owned and readying ourselves for this assault. We had sent word to the settlements of Balsheer, Melvais and Hamlin to tell them what was coming, and they had sent many of their young women to help us, with the understanding that we not put them in direct danger. Several of our households took in strangers in place of the children and old women who were leaving. As our big stone barn was cleared of animals, tack and valuables, it was turned into a dormitory for our guests.

I worried for Namuri in all this. She looked so thin and haggard that I feared for her health, and yet she never stopped moving. The thing that was hardest for her and that I think caused her most stress was trying to get the children and old women safely out of Nessian. Most of them didn't want to go, the children because they thought they would be missing something, the old women because they felt useless and pushed aside.

I was on my way home one morning when I saw our neighbor, Garnith, arguing with her granddaughter in front of their house. Ishta had thrown down her bundle and was shouting, "I won't go! Nothing exciting ever goes on here. Now when something is actually going to happen, you want to send me away."

Namuri and Lucian were coming down the street at that moment, leading a group of children, so they were witness to this outburst. Before Garnith could even say a word, Namuri had commanded in her sternest voice, "Ishta, apologize to your grandmother and hug her goodbye. Do you think this is some sort of entertainment you're being deprived of? This is serious business and those of us who stay may all be dead before it's over. We're trying to save your life. You will go where you're told to go, do what you're told to do and help where you're told to help. That's an order. Now pick up your bundle and come with me."

Looking awed and frightened, Ishta obeyed. By that afternoon the first wagonload of children, older women and supplies was leaving for the hills.

I was also there when Senli's great-grandmother refused to go. "I would rather die in my bed than out there camped in the woods. They have taken my Senli, the joy of my life, my only great-granddaughter. They have killed my future. They may as well take me too, kill this old body right here if it pleases them. I'm not going anywhere."

I saw the look of distress on Namuri's face but also her determination. "I'm sorry for this disrespect, Mother, but you leave me no choice." Then she ordered me to help Senli's mother carry the old woman out to the waiting wagon and lay her gently down among the mats and pillows.

It was Josian, a stranger I had just met on the road, who became our main organizer in everything, rather than Namuri. Josian seemed to be everywhere at once, giving commands, packing or re-packing wagons, checking supplies. Several times I heard her apologize to Namuri, saying, "I'm sorry. You are Headwoman here and I seem to be giving orders. I don't mean to be usurping your place."

Finally Namuri said impatiently, "It's fine, Josian. Don't hesitate and don't apologize! Just get on with it! Say whatever you think needs to be done and we'll try to do it. And please don't say 'sorry' to me again. It gets tiresome. You've lived in the world out there and know better what to do. This is way past my experience or abilities. I'm not offended. I'm just grateful you're willing to stay and help us."

At that Josian stopped in her rush and said with sudden seriousness, "I have to tell you, Namuri, I'm not just doing this for you and for this settlement. All of the West Country is at risk if these men begin raiding here. Up to now even the city of Hernorium has held to the old pact. They've started raiding east but never come west before. I don't want to see the peace broken and armies marching through this part of the world again. I'm every bit as determined to resist as Karil and Adana. I just have different methods. Hopefully we can all come out of this alive."

The core of our plan was an ambush. We had to find a way of drawing Peltron and his men into a place where we could trap, control and disarm them without all getting ourselves killed in the process. We had the perfect place for such a piece of work, but we were loath to use it for that purpose. It was a place most of us considered sacred. Also it was much too close to the settlement. That was a good thing in some ways because then we would have easy access and be able to make everything ready ahead of time without any chance of interference. It was a bad thing because we were afraid the violence could easily spill over into Nessian itself.

We called this place The Grove, or Evandaru's Chamber, or The Sacred Place. About two miles from the settlement the road forked. Nessian lay to the right on the larger road. The fork to the left was a narrower way and went deeper into the woods. After another mile or so it passed between two huge rock mounds, almost like small hills, called by us Hawk Rock and Owl Rock because of their suggestive shapes. They were like a gateway to the clearing, making a fairly narrow entry to the space and giving it a sense of separateness, the feeling of a place set apart. The top of those rock mounds was a perfect observation place, as well as a good place from which to roll down boulders in order to close the opening. Beyond those two rock outcroppings there was a line of other large rocks on either side of the grove, almost like a wall, though not one made by human hands. The road continued to a way out at the other end, but again not a wide passage and one that could easily be blocked ahead of time. If the entry was closed off, it would seem to be a trap with no way out, but between the rocks on the left there was a narrow opening that no one was likely to find unless they already knew it was there. That could be the escape route for our horses. The center of the grove was a small clearing, mostly grass and moss with the trees lining either side nearer to the rocks. There could hardly be a better spot for an ambush, but it had raised a heated argument, being both the best place and worst place we could have found.

"How could you even think to use The Grove that way? Maybe even shed blood there? Bring all that evil energy into our sacred space?"

"Because clearly there's no better place. It's almost as if it was made for that very purpose. I know of no other place that has such useful natural features. If you do, then you should say so and we can go look at it rather than sit here crossing words with each other."

"Aren't you afraid Evandaru will turn her back on us if we use her sacred space that way?"

"It feels as if She's already turned her back."

"Perhaps She'll help us protect it."

"How can you think of bringing men there, especially hostile ones?"

This debate went on and on, long enough to give me a headache and a terrible bout of impatience, long enough to wish myself somewhere else. I had forgotten how argumentative we could be. Sometimes I wished Namuri would just tell us what to do so we could get on with doing it without all the endless discussions, but of course that would never have worked. Namuri knew better. She was not a Magistrar. She did not give orders. She was our peacekeeper, the one who held us on course, the one who kept us to our better selves. She knew she only ruled by consent, not force. Before we could give our consent we had to be committed to the course of action, and before we could be committed we had to discuss every aspect of the situation to the point of boredom or madness.

In this sensitive matter Josian stayed in the background and allowed Namuri to guide us through. In the end, although the thought of doing such bloody work in sacred space sickened me, the practicality of it won out. I finally had to give my consent along with all the others who objected, since none of us could propose a better place or a better plan.

After that Josian divided us into four groups: riders, waiters, watchers and caretakers. The riders would be in charge of leading Peltron and his men into the trap by going out and engaging

74

them, appearing and disappearing, teasing and taunting, making sure to be followed while at the same time staying out of danger. She particularly emphasized that last part—staying out of danger. "We don't need to have anyone hurt." The waiters would be hidden in and around the grove, ready to take action there. The watchers would hide in the hills just above Nessian, keeping watch on the settlement and ready to do whatever was needed there. And the caretakers would be in charge of the very old women, the children and the animals, older women themselves who could not be so active but could cook and manage the camp.

I, of course, became one of the riders, as did many of the other young women in Nessian, those who were best on horseback, Karil and Adana among them. We would be the ones to draw Peltron and his men into following us, especially me since I was to be the main bait in our trap. None of the women from other settlements were allowed to become riders because of the danger, except for Nadir who insisted and who was already a friend and well known to several of us. "I have a right to ride with you. Those were my good friends Peltron stole out of the woods just as they were coming home from visiting me. I want to do whatever I can to stop him."

Josian gave her a stern look. "As long as you do nothing foolish, nothing on your own, especially nothing in the heat of vengeance which always makes one both foolish and careless. If this is to work we must each do our part perfectly, no mistakes, no crossing each other up. Understood?"

Nadir nodded. "Understood."

In one corner of the big barn there was a heap of old metal, left over from broken plows and the like, things we were always meaning to repair or re-make into something useful. Out of this tangle of discards we cut and shaped and sharpened long pieces of metal, bound on handles in leather for a firm grip and easy holding, and fashioned the whole thing into what Josian called swords, but what really looked to me like very long knives. After all I had seen real swords in the city of Hernorium and these hardly met their measure. When I said that to Josian, she told me to keep my silence on it. "Let the women here think of them as swords. It will give them confidence. These blades are already as long as they can handle. At least each woman will have something for defending herself." After all the riders had swords, she kept some of our women hard at work, making more. She wanted as many of us armed as possible. "You never know what may be needed," she said several times.

Every day Josian had her "riders" out in the field, teaching us how to slash and parry with sticks and then wooden blades before using real metal, working us until our arms ached and our backs were screaming. When we felt comfortable enough with our swords she set us to stabbing at straw men held up by branches. She also taught us to ride in a whole new way. Not that Josian herself was much of a horsewoman. Almost any of us was a better rider, but she had knowledge of the world. She knew what we needed to learn if we were going to survive. Also she had great skill at organization and command. Though stern and unrelenting, she was also very fair. We learned to trust her. Anyhow, there was no one among us who could have done this any better. Certainly not Namuri, who would come and watch for a while, her face drawn and pinched with worry and her eyes sad, before she would go away again, shaking her head. And not Lucian either. She didn't know enough of the world. Nor would any of us have been eager to follow her, not with her sharp tongue and abrasive ways.

I thought I was skilled on horseback, but this sort of riding was very different from anything I knew and I had to pick myself up off the ground several times. Hard to admit, but Karil, who had always envied my ability with horses, learned faster and did much better at it. She enjoyed letting me know this through little covert looks and cutting remarks.

Josian had us set up a course of barrels, flagged poles and other obstacles, and we were to weave through them at top speed, maneuvering between them as close as possible without actually touching. Then, when we mastered that, straw men were set up along the way for us to skewer in passing. My big horse Sand was different from little Mercy in every possible way. Tall and rangy and a lover of speed, he had no patience for weaving between obstacles when it was so much easier, faster and more pleasurable to run flat out right past them. After a while he came to understand the game of it and played as well as any of the others. Before that, to everyone's amusement, he threw me off sideways a few times when I wanted him to turn and he had already decided to go straight ahead. Once, when he threw me, I sat there for a while stunned, unable to move. It was Karil who helped me up, the only one who noticed my fall. It might have looked like an act of kindness, but as she gave me her hand she leaned forward and said in my ear, "If you're such a good rider, why are you always ending up with your rear end on the ground?" Then she gave me a quick sharp smile that was full of malice.

I said nothing, too heartsick to answer. I just took Sand's reins and limped home. Elani was working in our garden. She saw the look on my face and came to sit by me on the stoop. I felt bruised and weary, old, my bones aching. I knew I was getting more skilled every day, learning new things, but in truth I wanted none of it. I just wanted to be home in peace: planting the garden, feeding the goats, swimming in the river, walking in the woods, visiting with friends—and, most of all, riding for the pleasure of it, not because my life depended on my skill. Also I wanted to be making love with Adana, but at the moment that seemed like only a distant dream. Instead I was risking my bones every day learning how to ride like an acrobat, nothing I would have chosen to do, and how to swing a sword I could not imagine using against human flesh. As I shut my eyes I could feel tears leaking from the corners of them.

Elani put her arm around my shoulders and drew me close. I sighed and leaned against her. "Why does she hate me so?"

She didn't have to ask who. "I don't think she hates you. It's just that she doesn't love herself very much." She was silent for such a long while I thought that was the end of it, she wasn't going to say any more. I could feel her sadness almost as if it were my own. Finally she sighed and went on, "Of course, our 'chosen children' are always someone else's unwanted ones. Sometimes they learn to love, most of the time in fact, but sometimes they don't, they've already been too damaged. As you know she was almost two when she came to us and you were already three, always the big sister, always ahead of her, always out of reach.

"Who knows what had already happened in her young life. I doubt she remembers, but I can only think it wasn't good. She was such a sad little thing with those big dark eyes. I fell in love with her the moment I set eyes on her and just had to bring her home. Marn wasn't so sure. Children were something new in her life since she herself never had much chance to be a child. Dealing with one child was enough of a challenge for her, maybe more than enough, but I was very determined. Karil and Marn did become friends after a while. She used to follow Marn all over, sounding like a little bird, calling out, 'Marnie, Marnie, wait, I come wif you.'

"Karil's right that I hadn't wanted to birth any more children. I certainly didn't try for another one. Too much effort and too uncertain. The whole enterprise must be planned for and thought about and carefully considered. In the outside world they have far too many children, more than they can care for, more than they want. They don't know how to stop them from coming. And we have too few. For us it's not easy to have a child. The trip to the city of Tremorn, the waiting for your time, the difficulty of the procedure and not even knowing if it will take, the fear that it might be a boy that you would just end up losing and breaking your heart over.

"If I hadn't seen her, looking so much like she needed a mother, I would probably have just stopped at one child. Karil always thought I loved you best because you were the child of my body. But I picked her out. I chose her, I loved her, I adored her. I knew I would birth no more children and so she was to be my last one. But she was always angry and kept pushing me away. Finally I gave up. It was too painful trying to love her, like trying to love against a knife blade or trying to hug a cactus."

"And Grandmother Orlin, was she also a chosen child?"

She shook her head and laughed, a little sadly. "Oh no, not at all. As fate would have it, just the opposite. She was the birth child and her three sisters were 'chosen children.' They were very close because they felt they only had each other in the world, and she felt shut out by them. Because of my mother I worked so hard to make sure Karil knew she was loved and wanted. No matter how hard I tried, though, she never believed it. You, on the other hand, always knew I loved you, even when I neglected you a little for Karil's sake. And so you see, no matter what you do you never really know how things will turn out. Your grandmother and your sister are a great mystery to me."

After that we fell into a companionable silence. I could have sat with her the rest of the afternoon, but I knew I had to drag my weary, aching body back to the practice field. There was still more to learn.

When we had mastered everything to Josian's satisfaction, she had us practice mounting and dismounting at a run. Finally she taught us how to get another woman up on our horse while in motion. Next we had to train our horses in the grove, teaching them how to dash in at top speed and then vanish through the gap between the stones as soon as we slipped off their backs. She also had us take them into the woods and move as fast as possible through the trees. After that she thought us ready for almost anything.

At the end of a long, hot, sweaty day, Josian assembled all her riders. "Well, to the best of my ability I've taught you everything you need for defending yourselves or at least everything I know. Now our time must be almost up. You have to make ready to leave soon." Then, hands on hips, she looked us up and down slowly and critically. "I have to say, for a bunch of farmers you make passable warriors, better than I might have imagined." I wasn't sure if this was actually slight praise or a sideways insult.

After that she chose two from among us, Morith and Wanuil, to be our leaders based on what she had observed of their skills. I had always known Morith to be fair and kind and levelheaded, but I wasn't so happy about her choice of Wanuil. I had bad memories of her from my childhood as a bully and a tease. Since growing up I had mostly avoided her. She had been particularly cruel when Marn had left, tormenting us about having only one mother. "Guess you're both so ugly you drove her away, or maybe your mother smells bad."

For once on the same side, Karil and I exchanged a look of silent understanding, and she made an ugly face behind Wanuil's back. Well, we would just have to make the best of it. Josian had our new leaders drill us for another day or so while she watched. By then we supposed that our time was up.

When we were ready to leave, the whole settlement poured out to see us off and wish us luck. None of us knew if we would ever see each other again. Elani was not at all happy to have both her daughters in the riding party, going off into such danger. I tried my best to reassure her, though I myself was very well aware of the dangers. Karil just shrugged her off rudely. At that moment I really missed Marn and wished she was there to comfort our mother. As we rode off I was full of fear but excitement and anticipation at the same time. I wondered if this was how men felt when going into battle.

We set up camp a day's ride from Nessian. From there we sent out four women on our fastest horses to scout ahead while we waited, playing games of chance to make the time pass. Two of them stayed out there to keep watch on the men, and the other two, Rialin and Fedra, rode back to report that, at the pace they were moving, Peltron and his men were less than two days away from us. "There are about sixty of them, well armed, and two large supply wagons, all moving slowly. They seem very confident, spread out across the road and with no sentries. I'm sure they didn't see us, but they're easy enough to spot with all the dust they're making——and all the noise. Right now they're going through Sharnum Valley, too open, not a good place for an encounter, but by the time we can meet up with them they'll be back in the deep woods again."

We set out immediately but kept to a slow, steady pace, not

wanting to tire our horses. That was the last real camp we would make and the last hot food we would eat. No more campfires that might give away our location. We each carried enough dried food in our knapsacks to cover our needs for the next few days. We had to be able to move rapidly and with ease, faster than armed men with wagons.

It was on the morning of the second day that we actually met up with them. Rialin was right. Even through the trees we could see the cloud of dust they raised well before we could see the men. Soon we could hear their loud voices.

Our first encounter was intended to be very quick, just barely showing ourselves. We waited at the end of a long straight stretch of road for them to come around a corner. When they appeared we watched for Morith's signal. As soon as she raised her arms we rode straight at them, shouting and howling. It was important that I be seen since I was the target of all this, the bait in the trap, so to speak. Just before we turned I rode a few steps past the others and yelled, "Peltron, you flea-bitten dog, you lost me once, you won't catch me again!" Then I shook my head vigorously to make sure he caught the flash of my red hair. After that I spun Sand around and sent him into a gallop, glad for all the training we had shared together. Not waiting to hear Peltron's curses, the rest of our riders whirled about and thundered down the road after me. I let Rialin pass me and she quickly led us off the road and onto a narrow path she knew. We all vanished into the forest before they could even mount a pursuit.

When we finally stopped, I slipped off Sand's back and leaned against him, laughing and sobbing with relief. We had taken them totally by surprise. It was a while before we heard the sound of their horses galloping down the road and later galloping back.

On those first few raids the plan was just to appear and disappear, making a lot of noise and galloping off before we could be touched. We were faster than they were and more mobile, having no wagons to haul, as well as no heavy armor or weapons. Also we knew how to appear and disappear, vanishing up secret little paths. After all, this was our world they were intruding into.

But, of course, they would be ready for us now and the game would get even more dangerous. And there were other risks besides those men. In one of those mad dashes off the road and into the woods, Adana's horse stumbled on a root and she was thrown, falling against a rock and injuring her leg so that she walked with a limp. I saw her wince with pain each time she set weight on her foot, but when I showed concern she just shrugged and told me to let her be.

Since we kept being successful each time, we began getting more daring with our raids, perhaps even foolish or careless. It was very frightening but also more exciting than anything else in the lives of young women who had grown up in an isolated settlement with little change in their daily routine. I suppose it almost seemed like a game to some. They really had no idea what these men were capable of doing.

Our next foray was to be at night, a raid on Peltron's camp, something they probably wouldn't be expecting. Our instructions were to ride just one time around the camp screaming and shouting and then be gone as quickly as possible into the darkness. We circled around as we were supposed to, but Ayair, usually shy and quiet, must have felt especially daring that night or perhaps she wanted to impress Karil who was riding next to her and for whom she clearly felt an attraction. With a loud yell, Ayair made a wild dash straight across the camp, probably intending to jump the fire. Then her horse, going at full speed, stumbled over a saddle on the ground and she was pitched over his head. The closest man made a grab for her arm and gave a roar of triumph when he had her.

I thought for sure Ayair was gone, lost to us. If we delayed leaving, they might have us all. None of us was close enough to save her except Karil. With a loud shout and without a moment's hesitation, Karil rushed in after Ayair, her sword slashing right and left. The man who held Ayair scrambled out of Karil's way and other men leapt back with shouts of surprise as Karil grabbed Ayair's arm, dragged her across the circle and hauled her up on her horse's neck, shouting to the rest of us, "Out of here now!"

Men leapt up to follow us and we had to ride hard to get away. After a few bends in the road we turned and followed Rialin down one of our secret little paths. Very soon we heard the men thundering past us, much too close for comfort. If not for the cover of darkness, they might well have seen where we left the road. Ayair, very frightened by her close call, finally managed to sit up in front of Karil, holding the horse's mane with one hand. After a while her horse caught up to us. She was able to remount with Karil's help, but she groaned with pain. The arm that Karil had dragged her with hung at a strange painful-looking angle, probably dislocated. She kept thanking Karil for saving her life and the rest of us also praised Karil for her courage and quick-wittedness, all except Wanuil who kept muttering about one fool rushing in to save another.

As soon as it was clear that we were safe, we stopped and dismounted to deal with Ayair's injury. Wanuil was threatening to pull it back in place herself, and I shuddered to think of Ayair in such rough hands. She would certainly not be gentle. She had already said several times how angry she was. "Such an idiot! Did you think yourself clever? Were you showing off for us or for those men?"

I was glad to see Nadir step forward at that moment. "Let me have a look at it. I know something of healing." She felt gently up and down the arm while Ayair groaned and gritted her teeth. "Not so bad. Dislocated, not broken. I can put it back in place, but I need help. Solene, you hold her. Morith, put your hand over her mouth when I pull so she doesn't cry out." Then she leaned toward Ayair and said gently, "You may have been foolish, but you were also very brave. Now you will have to be brave again but just for a moment. As soon as it's back in place it will stop hurting."

"Don't talk so much about it," Ayair said through gritted teeth in a voice hoarse with pain. "Just do it and do it fast!"

And so, by the light of one candle held in Karil's hand, Nadir set Ayair's arm while I held her tightly and Morith kept a hand over her mouth to silence her cry. I could hear her shoulder pop back into place, could almost feel in my own body the sharp jolt of pain and then the easing of it. Ayair groaned again but this time with relief. "Thank you! Thank you! Now I can move my arm again."

"Don't move it too much. It was badly dislocated and needs to be kept still for a while so it doesn't slip out again." After Nadir had bound Ayair's arm against her body, making a rough sling out of a torn shirt, Wanuil said angrily, "So stupid! Whatever possessed you to do such a thing? No sense. You're out of here by first light, on the way home as fast as you can go. Lucky you weren't cut to pieces. Lucky Karil wasn't hacked up or captured getting you out. She was the only one in a position to save you. None of the rest of us could have done it. Just think what those men would have done to you. You've endangered us all by your recklessness. Why do you think Josian assigned you leaders? It was so you could obey orders, not go chasing off on wild schemes of your own."

Ayair hung her head and looked away during all this, not even trying to defend herself. Personally I thought she had endured enough already, but then Morith added, "This isn't a game, you know, Ayair, even if it may seem so at times. This is deadly serious and you were indeed a fool." Then, in a different tone, she went on, "As it is, we can make use of you. You will go back to Nessian with news and tell them to expect the raid tomorrow or the next day. Adana will go with you."

"Why me?" Adana asked quickly.

"Because I am your leader and I told you to. Also because you have an injured leg, so you're already slowed down and at risk. And besides that Ayair can't go alone with a hurt arm—much too dangerous."

Karil said quickly, "Perhaps I should go too and help." In the candlelight I could see her expression of naked love and longing as she looked at Adana. If I hadn't been so angry I might have felt sorry for her—or even embarrassed for her sake.

"No!" Wanuil said sharply. "Bad enough we lose two of our number due to Ayair's stupidity. We don't need to lose three because you're pining for your sister's lover." There was a glitter of malice in Wanuil's eyes, and I had the satisfaction of seeing Karil blush and turn away.

We only had one more quick encounter on the road with those men. It went uneventfully and according to plan. Once we got them chasing us, we disappeared again before they could get close. After that we sent Fedra ahead with word to make everything ready in the grove, then rode toward home and our last fateful meeting. We waited for the men about two miles or so from the fork in the road. We were close to the road, but well hidden by high shrubs. Rialin was watching for us up in a tree. When she thought them near enough she gave a shout.

We all poured out onto the road, close enough to be clearly seen but not so close as to really be in danger. I glanced back quickly. Several times since we started our raids I thought I had seen Torvin among Peltron's men. This time I was sure. Hard to believe he would come on such an ugly mission. Clearly I didn't know him as well as I thought I did. Even more surprising, I was sure I spotted Ramule riding next to his father. I was amazed that Peltron would bring his son—not much more than a boy really—on such a dangerous mission, but I suppose he thought he was teaching Ramule to be a man. No doubt Peltron expected us to be easy prey, good for sharpening his son's teeth. I hoped they were all in for a big surprise, but there was no time now to be thinking about Ramule—or Torvin either for that matter. We each had to do our own part of this work just right if we were going to survive the day.

As soon as we passed the fork in the road I heard Peltron's voice in back of me. He yelled out some names and then shouted furiously, "Go! That way! Set fire to everything you see and kill anything that moves. Then come back here and help me finish off these women."

Clearly he had given up any idea of capturing us alive and taking us back to the city for use. Far too much trouble, I suppose. Also we had wounded his pride with our raids. Now he wanted us dead and the whole settlement of Nessian dead along with us, burned to the ground, nothing left. No time to grieve for that now. No way I could stop them. We had done our best to get them all to follow us the whole way. Whatever was going to happen in the village would happen without me. I could only try to do my part here.

Moving at a run we paired up and poured through the pass, going two at a time as had been planned so as not to clog the opening in a sudden mass of confusion and tangled horses. It was not a moment too soon. They were right on our heels. Having left their wagons, they were galloping flat out, shouting and lashing their horses for even more speed, surely they were really going to catch up to us this time.

As Peltron charged in with his men, each woman rode as fast as she could to her chosen tree, grabbed the knotted rope left hanging there for her use and swung herself up into the branches, just as we had practiced so many times. At the same time our horses rushed off to disappear into the hidden gap between the stones, exactly as they had been trained to do. I paused for just a moment longer in the clearing so Peltron would be sure to see me, looking alone and undefended, before I sent Sand dashing after the others. When I went to swing up into my tree, as I had done countless times before, my foot slipped for some unknown reason, momentarily making me lose my grip on the knot. The rope I was dangling from began slipping painfully through my sweaty hands, and I saw myself ending up under his horse's hooves with Peltron's sword stuck in my back.

Other riders were screaming at me to move. I could hear Peltron's shout of triumph, thinking he surely had me. At the very last moment my grip held, and I was able to haul myself up onto a branch, clumsy, sweaty, panting with exertion and very frightened. As quickly as I could I pulled my rope up behind me. Peltron's shout of glee turned into a roar of rage as I seemed to vanish right before his eyes. He came so close I could feel the rush of wind from his horse's passing and I swear I could feel the horse's heat as well. I certainly saw the flash of his blade. He tried to stop, but he was going too fast and there were too many riding hard right behind him. No room to turn and come after me. I was shaking so hard I almost lost my grip on the tree. *No time for that now. Get yourself together,* I told myself sternly. *You have to be ready for whatever comes next.*

With a quick look around I saw that the others were all safely up in their trees with their ropes pulled up after them. When I glanced at the top of Hawk Rock, I was startled to see that it was Adana standing there, very still, not Eldrin whom I had expected to see. They must have changed plans when Adana came home early. Yora was on top of Owl Rock, also perfectly still. There were others standing behind each of them, dark shadows, waiting.

Meanwhile the men were pouring into our trap, galloping hard. I had a breathless moment of hope, thinking we had succeeded, thinking everything would go as planned and we would win our little battle here without too much damage, thinking we just needed to carry out the last part of our plan and soon could gather them all in like fish in a net. Then, from the rear of their charge, one of Peltron's men shouted, "A trap! It's a trap!" Instantly several others echoed his words. With that the forward surge began to slow and waver, and I knew in my bones, knew with terrible certainty, what would happen next and that it would not be good.

I heard Adana yelling, "The rocks! Roll the rocks!" With that the shadows behind her leapt into action. Next came the terrible grinding, screeching sounds of rocks moving against rocks and then crashing loudly as one after the other dropped into the gap, followed by the shouts and screams of men and horses trapped in the rockfall. I shuddered, sickened by the sound.

But we had no choice, I told myself. *We had to close the trap or all those men would have flowed out again just as quickly as they had flowed in. Then everything would have been lost, all our lives in danger with no way to win.* But for just a moment I thought, *we never meant to kill them, that wasn't part of the plans, not the men and certainly not the horses.*

Then everything was happening at once and there was no

time to think, only time to act. Someone else—Yora, I think—
was shouting, "Light the fires! Light the fires!" *Fires! Fires! Fires!*
The word echoed down the field and at almost the same moment
fire flared out all around and smoke began pouring up in dark,
acrid-smelling clouds, stinging the eyes and choking the breath.
Quickly I pulled a scarf from my belt to cover my nose and
mouth. It was only falsefire mixed with pitch that we had spread
in lines across the clearing. Making far more light and smoke
than heat, it was nonetheless terrifying to anyone not expecting
it. We had laid the mixture down in a zigzag pattern to break
up their charge and separate the men into manageable clumps
kept apart by lines of fire. Now the grove echoed with shouts of
surprise and fear as horses began rearing, throwing their riders.
Soon flames started shooting up everywhere, creating panic and
concealing the way out in billowing smoke.

I had just one moment to glance up at Adana. She had
stepped forward and was standing, arms raised, on the highest of
the rocks above me, glorious and terrifying, with flames flashing
out all around her, even from her hair and arms, magnificent
and beautiful in an unearthly way. She was screaming, "Off your
horses! Drop your weapons! Drop your weapons now or you will
all die! Off your horses now!" Some of the men had turned and
were gaping up at this fearful apparition, pointing, eyes wide with
fear. Meanwhile a terrible, eerie screeching had begun, coming
from all directions, followed by a discordant pounding of drums
that quickly grew louder and louder, a wave of sound to stab the
ears and bludgeon the mind. Other voices instantly took up the
cry, "Drop your weapons now! If you want to live, drop your
weapons and get off your horses now!"

The screeching was getting louder and more terrifying by
the moment. Flames were flaring up all across the grove. For
just an instant I thought I saw Peltron's white terrified face and
felt a rush of bitter joy at his fear, but when I heard again the
screams of men and horses trapped under the fallen rocks, my
satisfaction evaporated. This wasn't about vengeance. I had a job
to do. Peltron was only part of it. Through the pall of smoke I

saw some of his men drop their swords and raise their hands in surrender or plug their ears with their fingers to shut out the mind-numbing noise. The rest were hesitating, looking around in confusion as if for guidance. Then I heard Adana's voice again, "Get Peltron! Get Peltron! After that the others will be easy."

Moments later I saw Peltron himself materialize out of the smoke and fire, horseless, swordless and surrounded by armed women. Fedra had him by the arm. She was shaking him hard and shouting in his face, "Say it! Say it now, Peltron! Say it now!" Good thing that we had our little homemade swords to back up our words.

Peltron's face was twisted in anger. He hesitated as if considering resistance. Then, over all the noise and confusion his voice rang out, ragged with smoke and fury, "Put down your weapons, men! Surrender now!" After that a few men dropped their swords and then more and more of them, faster and faster, raising their hands and calling out, "Truce!" until it looked as though most of the men had surrendered. Finally the grove was a sea of waving hands, appearing and disappearing through the shifting smoke. One of the men who had not yet dropped his sword launched himself straight at Fedra as if he meant to run her through. I shouted a warning. Before he could do any harm, several women brought him down and he vanished under a sea of bodies. After that there was no more resistance.

It was over! Women all around me began shouting and cheering, a huge wave of sound that swept through the grove and went on and on. To those men it must have seemed almost as frightening as those other sounds we had made. I tried adding my voice, but it came out hoarse and hesitant. I was still too frightened by my close brush with Peltron's sword to feel much like cheering.

As soon as it seemed safe, those of us in the trees swung down on our ropes and dropped to the ground. Other women were quickly coming out of hiding at the edge of the trees, pouring into the clearing. Some were also coming through the gap between the rocks with more ropes and buckets of water. All were armed with swords and most had scarves over their faces.

The mind-numbing sound of drumming and screeching was finally fading away. By now we far outnumbered the invaders. Most of them were off their horses. Coughing, choking with smoke, they were looking around in bewilderment, dazed and confused as if they couldn't quite imagine how all this had happened to them so quickly. After all, they had come here as conquerors, with every assurance that they were going to destroy our village and kill or capture our women. Nothing could have prepared them for this turn of events, a good thing for us or we might never have succeeded. Everything we did had depended on surprise.

Since the lines of falsefire had divided the men into small groups, we began tying them together in bunches with long ropes. Weaponless and with Peltron captured, they gave us little argument, only a few curses and grumbles. I knew from my own experience that rope wouldn't hold them for long, but at least it would give us some advantage for now so we could gather up their armor and weapons and make them less of a threat.

In all this confusion, Ramule tried to run off. I saw the motion out of the corner of my eye. Before I could even say anything or move in that direction Josian was shouting, "Get the boy. Don't let him get away. That's Ramule, Peltron's son, the Magistrar's grandson."

Ramule was quickly captured. When he was brought back and tied with a group of other prisoners, Peltron called out, almost pleading, "Don't hurt him. He's only a boy. He's not the one responsible. He had nothing to do with this. I made him come."

By now Namuri had appeared on the scene. She was staring hard at Peltron, shaking her head. Then she pointed her cane at him. "So you're the arrogant fool who caused us all this pain and trouble. Hard to imagine. You don't look like much. No need to worry about the boy. We have no intention of harming him. We know well enough who's responsible here."

Peltron was straining against the rope, face turning red with anger. "If any harm comes to him we'll come back next time with a whole army of..."

"Enough!" Namuri shouted. I don't think I'd ever heard her shout before. Then in a calmer voice, but one with iron in it, she added, "I said we wouldn't harm him and you have my word on it. Right now, in case you hadn't noticed, Peltron, you're in no position to be making threats. It would be much better if you kept your silence."

When Namuri spoke in that voice of authority people listened, they had no choice. At her tone even Peltron ceased his threats, spluttering to a mumble and then silence. At that moment Josian stepped forward. "Good that the boy is here, Namuri. Peltron was a fool to bring him. He may be a very valuable playing piece in this ugly game, the key to it all. We can use him to bend his father's will."

Instantly Peltron turned his anger and frustration on Josian.

"Josian, the Woman Wagoner, how interesting to find you here. So you're the one behind all this trickery. These women could never have thought of all this by themselves. Believe me, you won't be able to fool us again with your fire-tricks. I always told Torvin you weren't to be trusted, that you shouldn't be allowed into the Palace. Don't think to show your face in Hernorium again, not unless you want to find it on the end of a pike."

She shrugged. "We all worked on the plan together. They may be country women, that doesn't make them fools. But no matter, I hadn't expected to come back to your city anyhow. Your loss, I'd say. I carry good wares."

With that Josian turned her back and walked away as if she didn't care, but I had seen the sadness in her face, I knew how much her friends in Hernorium meant to her. She quickly busied herself elsewhere, ordering some of the men freed so they could begin prying with long poles and metal bars, trying to move the boulders that blocked the passage. She sent them under guard with armed women so they wouldn't try to cause trouble or escape, not that they were likely to do any such thing in their present state. In fact they looked cowed and beaten down, cringing away when any of us approached them. Confused and purposeless, they still turned to Peltron for orders as if he was not as much a prisoner as they were.

"Get those rocks out of there and be quick about it!" he told his men, barking out commands as if he was still in charge. "We need to free those men and horses that are still alive!" Under the lash of his voice, his men began to move to their work with a little more purpose and energy.

Most of the flames had died back by now but smoke was still rising from the burning grass. Through the haze it was hard to distinguish one prisoner from the other, especially since they were all smeared with soot and ash, but there was one I needed to find. I went from one cluster to the next, looking for Torvin. Finally I found him, tied to some other men, quite close to the tree that had been my perch.

"What are you doing here?" I growled. "What kind of fool are you anyway? Don't you know you could have been killed, crushed under those rocks?" I was incredibly relieved to see him alive and unharmed and at the same time furious at him. And on top of that, altogether amazed at how much I cared, how much it mattered to me. "How could you do that?" I shouted at him. "How could you come with Peltron on such a foul venture? I thought you were better than that."

He reached out to put a hand on my arm, pulling against the rope that bound him. At the same time the man tied next to him tried to pull the other way, clearly frightened of me, especially in my anger. "I was afraid for you, Solene. I know my brother, know his harsh ways, what he's capable of doing. I thought if I came I could prevent the worst from happening, perhaps even save your life. I was afraid if he caught up with you he might be angry enough to kill you." Then he glanced around and gave a wry laugh. "Maybe I was protecting the wrong person."

At that I laughed too and suddenly we both were laughing together, quite inappropriately, in sheer relief from the tension of the day. The man next to him began to curse and shout, tugging back on the rope and yelling to be set free. I quickly stepped over to him, hand raised to cuff him. Just in time I realized what I was doing, dropped my hand and said reasonably, "Be patient. You'll be able to go when all this is sorted out. After all, we didn't invite you here."

I heard my name being called and started to leave, but I wasn't comfortable walking away and leaving Torvin tied. "I could release you if you gave me your word to stay."

He shook his head. "I can see you're not much good at battles. That's not what you're supposed to do. You're not supposed to set the enemy free. After all, that's what I am, I'm the enemy here."

"But you came here to save my life."

"How do you know? Just because I told you so? Don't believe everything people tell you, Solene, especially if they're the enemy. I'll just stay here with these men and share their fate until everything's decided. Surely you have other things you need to be doing rather than talking to me." I walked away reluctantly. When I looked back the smoke had hidden him from sight again.

Feeling somewhat lost, I was drawn toward the sound of raised voices. Namuri and Peltron were still arguing. Peltron's rough voice carried over the general commotion and I went in that direction. "What do you mean you won't care for the wounded? What are we to do with them? The ride back to the city is too long. They may die on the way."

Namuri was shaking her head. "Not our problem."

"And what about the dead? Surely you can't expect us to take them too? It's too hot. The bodies will begin to rot before we get back."

"Also not our problem. The little inconveniences of battle that you had hoped to leave for someone else to tend to? You should have thought of all that before you came here, in fact before you left home. Once more, Peltron, just so you clearly understand. No, we will not bury your dead. And no, we will not care for your wounded. We have enough to clear up here because of you. Did you go off on a raid not expecting any of your men to get hurt? Shortsighted, I'd say. Dead or wounded, take them all back in the wagons you came with, the ones you would have used for our women if you had succeeded in capturing us. When your men have moved away the rocks, we will untie you and give you back your sword, just for a moment. Then you can go over there, under guard, and decide who can be saved and who must die by your sword. Yours to choose, not our work to do."

The sound of Peltron's voice made me feel ill, but I couldn't walk away. I was drawn and repelled at the same time. My impulse was to run. Instead I stepped forward and snarled, "Take all of these men and all of this rubbish back to your cold, ugly city and never come near us again."

At that Peltron whirled around, his face soot-smeared, his eyes wild-looking and red with smoke. He was straining furiously against his bonds. "You're the one who caused me all this trouble in the first place," he shouted furiously at me.

Spluttering with outrage, I yelled back, "Not me! How can you say that? I didn't cause you any trouble. You're the one. You caused yourself and everyone else this trouble. I was just walking in the woods picking mushrooms. You came and snatched me away. You raped me, you beat me, you almost ruined my life. And now you want to blame me for what you did? You're lucky to be alive. Your son's lucky to be alive. So is your brother. We could have killed you all. Maybe we still will." My hand was on my knife, trembling, itching to strike. I was far too angry to be cautious.

Morith grabbed my arm and shook me, "Stop it, Solene! Get away from him! Things are already bad enough. Don't make them worse."

At that moment Ayair came galloping in through the newly opened gap, riding one-handed with her arm still bound to her chest. "Nessian is burning! We need help! Hurry!"

Furious, I lunged at Peltron with my knife. "You did this! I heard you give the order." I had the pleasure of seeing him cringe away, fear in his eyes as well as anger. Morith jerked my arm back, and Namuri said forcefully, "Go with them, Solene! Now! They need you and you need to be gone from here before you're the one who causes us more grief." She gave me a little push to break the spell of my anger and get me moving.

She was right. I needed to ride away quickly, out of range of that man's hateful voice. I ran to find Sand, threw myself on his back, and joined with the other women who were gathering to leave. I was afraid that if I stayed I might actually do Peltron some very personal injury with my newly found sword-skill and so ruin everything. For myself I wouldn't have regretted it, not for one moment. I could easily have stabbed him, even to death—no guilt and no regret. Time spent in his city had certainly hardened my heart. But such a rash action might have terrible consequences for us all, might even provoke a war well beyond the scope of this little raid.

Having seen enough of these men to last me a lifetime, I rode with the rest of the women, Nadir and Morith among them, back to the settlement, while the others stayed on in the grove to better secure the men, find and gather the horses and stack up the weapons and armor so they couldn't be used again. We rode hard, afraid of what we would find.

Soon we were met on the road by a group of men riding hard in the other direction. Their faces were soot-streaked, and they reeked of smoke. With a shock I realized that these had to be the men who had just set fire to Nessian. They hesitated as if they thought of attacking us right there on the road, though we easily outnumbered them. Then Morith shouted, "Peltron needs you. He's in terrible trouble." With that they swept by, lashing their horses for speed. I glanced back just once and at the same moment one of those men also glanced back. For just that instant our eyes met and locked in fury.

I could smell the smoke well before we got there and soon after that could hear the crackle of fire. Then we came around a bend in the road and I saw Nessian in flames. Nothing could have prepared me for the appalling sight that met my eyes or the stab of grief that ran through my heart like a sword. I could see my shock reflected on the faces of the others at the sight of our village burning. Peltron's men had ridden through and torched everything. Every house and shed and barn was on fire. I wasn't sure at that moment that I had made the right choice. Better to have stayed back there in the grove and cut up some of those men with my sword than to be facing this ruin. I had an irrational moment of anger at Josian for making us abandon the settlement to them. If Peltron had been standing in front of me, I could have easily killed him on the spot.

I thought it was all gone, everything, just as I had foreseen that day after the meeting. I was numb, frozen in place, my mind empty. All I could do was stare transfixed into the flames. Then Morith shouted at me, "Come on, Solene, move, we're here to help, not watch." With that I came back to myself and realized that things might not be as bad as they seemed at first. Though the roofs were on fire, some of the houses were still standing, at least those that were made of stone. Those men had only lit what would burn, not stayed to destroy the buildings. Finding no one there to kill—since our women had all been in hiding—they had torched what would burn, then quickly moved on to the scene of battle.

Now that my eyes had cleared I could see lines of women everywhere, hauling water from the wells and the pond, running with buckets, passing buckets, climbing ladders. My aunt Lucian seemed to be in charge. "Over here," she shouted. "We need help right here. Get off your horses and move! Now!"

There was no way to tie our horses where they wouldn't be in danger from the fire so we just let them loose. For a while I went mindlessly wherever I was told to go and did as I was ordered, carrying water or passing it on or pouring it on the fire, moving as fast as I could and hardly stopping to catch my breath. I worked in a daze. At some moment I suddenly realized it was our own house I was dousing with water. I hadn't even been aware of it. Then someone called me away and I went. Once I saw Elani, rushing by, staggering under the weight of two full buckets. I wanted to help, but at that moment I had to keep my place in the line.

The dried rushes from the roof thatch burned only too well. Sometimes a breeze would come through and there would be such a blast of heat we had to leap back. We were trying to put out the flames and save the rafters, though in most cases it was hopeless. After a while the fires began to abate. There was more smoke and steam and less flame.

Finally Lucian called a halt. For that moment at least, the fires seemed to be contained. Looking around the ruins of what had been our lives, we discovered it was not as bad as it had seemed at first. After all, our houses were largely made of mud and stone. Most of them, though damaged, were still standing. Small outbuildings, sheds and barns made of wood had burned down, but the biggest barn, off to the side, the one that was made of stone and roofed with slate tiles, hadn't been touched.

At Lucian's signal we all dropped our buckets and found ourselves staggering about, gasping, groaning, exhausted, bent over with coughing from the acrid smoke. My arms ached, my hands were cut and blistered, my hair and eyebrows singed. I had burns on my hands, my arms, my face, my legs, any part of me that was exposed. My clothes were torn, drenched and smoking. I was choking and my eyes were streaming. My companions, what was visible of them through the swirls of smoke and steam, seemed in much the same condition, though at that moment we could hardly see each other. Then a sudden breeze came up, the dark cloud lifted momentarily and there we all were, looking at each other in stunned disbelief, a band of hideous ghosts, the bedraggled survivors of a disaster.

Morith pointed at me and started to laugh, a harsh croaking sound that had little humor in it. "Solene, you look like something out of a bad dream."

I looked around and began pointing at the others, "Well, the rest of you don't look any better. Walking nightmares, that's what we all are. Even our own mothers wouldn't recognize us." I started to laugh too, that same raspy, choking, hideous sound and some of the others joined me.

Suddenly, over the sound of our rough laughter, we heard the pounding of horses' hooves and all spun around, frightened and ready to defend ourselves. The figure coming at us through the pall of smoke was certainly not one of our own. It had a sword in hand, raised as if for battle, and seemed intent on riding us down. As we each pulled our much smaller swords from our belts, Lucian shouted, "Get out of the way! Go to either side and surround him!"

At the sound of her voice the figure reined in its horse, lowered its sword and seemed to hesitate. I was amazed to hear *him* asking in a woman's voice, "What happened here?" With a cry, Elani dashed between our raised swords, flinging herself in the direction of the dark figure. At that the figure dropped its sword altogether, held up its hands and shouted in a voice that was strangely, achingly familiar. "It's me, Marn. Don't attack me! Put down your knives! Please! I thought you were raiders. What terrible thing has happened here?"

Without waiting for an answer Marn slid off her horse and ran to throw herself into Elani's open arms. They met halfway between, with a cry of joy. After that they hugged and separated to look at each other and then hugged again several more times as if none of the rest of us even existed. Finally they drew back, and Marn asked again, "What has happened? What have I come home to? Whatever it is, I'm grieved and shamed that I wasn't here to help you."

Interrupting each other, all our words tumbling out in a rush, we told her everything that had happened while Elani clung to her side as if she had just found the rest of herself, her second skin, and would never let it go again.

Gesturing at the smoking ruin all around us, Marn exclaimed, "But this is too terrible to believe. What of the contract? Have these men all gone mad? Do they care for nothing? And to think that I have come back at just this moment."

Then, shaking her head, she added regretfully, "I thought so many times of coming home. Is there still a place for me here, Elani, or have you found someone else? I know I have no right to ask. I stayed away year after year, meaning to come home and yet afraid to, afraid of finding no welcome here after the way I left. I was never happy there in that city, but I learned many things: how to work metal, how to play music, how to fight like a man. I've worked at cutting stone and shoeing horses and building huge buildings, passing for a man there because it was safer, but the loneliness finally got to me and drove me back, the loneliness of living in a place where I could never be my real self, a stranger in a city of strangers."

I had never heard Marn string together so many words at one time. I think she was trying to convince us she was worth taking back. I understood only too well her loneliness in the city. I had found city life unbearable after only a few days and she had been gone for seven years, a whole lifetime lived somewhere else. But of course she had come from that world to start with and also chosen to be in that city, not been snatched away against her will. We all crowded around her then, reaching out to touch her, to pet her, to hug her, to welcome her home.

Lucian had just said, "We need to get back quickly to the others," when Nadir shouted and pointed. Some of the roofs had begun flaring up again. We had to get back to our water buckets and make new lines, though it felt much harder now that we had stopped. As soon as it seemed safe we left several women there to guard against more fires, Marn and Elani among them, and rode as fast as possible back to the scene of battle where so much was yet to be decided.

When we got there, our horses sweaty and heaving from having been run the whole way, we found the entrance to the grove already open and most of the rocks cleared away. Four dead horses lay among the boulders. At first I mistook them for rocks. Then I noticed the blood and saw that their throats had been cut. Eyes burning with tears, I turned away and rode on. Those horses had no fault in this; they had not chosen to come here. The men we passed on the road had been disarmed and were loading the wagons with their dead and wounded while a group of our women guarded them. Looking frightened, they backed away in haste to let us ride through.

A meeting of sorts was already in progress, and I was amazed at the sight that met my eyes. We had left the grove a scene of total chaos and confusion and had come back to find everything in some sort of rough order. Josian appeared to be in charge of the organizing. There were several neat stacks of weapons and armor. Most of the horses had been collected on a long line and were grazing quietly as if nothing out of the ordinary had happened here. Men were all tied together in manageable bundles, five or six or seven together. Some had even mastered the cooperation required to sit down on the scorched grass. The falsefire had mostly gone out. There were only little wisps of smoke here and there and an occasional lick of flame, though the bitter smell of it still lingered in the air as a reminder of all that had happened.

In the middle of this strange scene I saw Ramule, tied to a tree, with an armed woman standing guard on either side of him. Glowering with what seemed to be anger or frustration, he appeared to be the center of everyone's attention. As I stared at him in surprise, a shaft of sunlight suddenly illuminated his face and then his whole figure so that he shone for a moment in golden light, casting everyone else in shadow. Nadir, riding next to me, sucked in her breath and said with a sort of awed amazement, "Isn't he beautiful?"

I was shocked at her words. Beautiful? Not hardly! Personally I could see nothing beautiful about him. To me this was still the same sullen arrogant face I had seen in Hernorium, only now it was tinged by fear. I saw nothing beautiful there. I looked at her in surprise and wondered what on earth she could be thinking.

Someone had put a saddle on the ground for Namuri to sit on, and she was speaking in a loud, clear voice, tapping with her cane to emphasize her words. "It's not complicated. It's really quite simple. The boy stays with us. His life is in your hands, Peltron. Do as we say and he will be returned to you safely and in good health. Go against our wishes and you forfeit his life. Killing him is not something we would do willingly, but something we are prepared to do if our terms are not met. First off, you must all go, all but Ramule. Leave no one skulking around. Not one man or that one is dead for sure and the boy also! We have gathered up your horses, as many as we could find. I'm glad to see that you're putting your wounded in your wagons even if it causes you some inconvenience. You brought them here; you get to take them home again. Be glad I restrained Solene or you yourself might be among the dead or wounded, instead of standing here arguing with us. She certainly has cause enough.

"Secondly, and pay close attention for this is most important, we want our own women, the three you stole, returned to us safely. No more than ten of you can come back with them. You must be unarmed and unarmored. You must not mistreat them in any way. You must get them out of slavery as soon as you get back and return here immediately. Then you can have your boy again and take him home. It's a bother to keep a hostage. We'll be only too glad to let you have him, but only if you do exactly as we say and are back here before the month is out. Otherwise we will have to..."

Impulsively I shouted, "And Banya and Dorial, if they want to come." I remembered Dorial's dislike of life in the city. "Let them come here and live free among us if that's what they want."

"And Banya and Dorial if they want to come," Namuri repeated.

Torvin said quickly, "Let me stay with the boy. I can be your second hostage. He's too young to be left here alone."

Namuri shook her head. "One hostage is as much as we can handle. He was old enough to come here as a soldier. He's old enough to stay as a hostage."

"Then take me in his place and let him go home. His mother will be frantic with worry."

Namuri was shaking her head. "All the better, all the more likely to bind his father's will."

"No, Torvin, you can't stay here," I interrupted hastily. "Go back to Hernorium. Find our sisters. It's up to you to gain their freedom, insure their safety and bring them back to us as quickly as possible. The faster that's done the faster Ramule can go home." With all my confused and conflicted feelings about him, I couldn't bear the thought of Torvin staying in Nessian as a captive and being a part of my life here.

"How do I know you'll treat him well?" Peltron asked in a menacing voice. I could see him try to take a threatening step forward but he was bound too tightly to the other men.

"After all you've done you have no right to ask, but yes, you can believe we'll treat him fairly because I say we will and I'm Headwoman here. You'll have to make do with that, my promise. The women of Nessian keep their word."

The sound of his voice brought back all my anger. I found my hand on my sword again, gripping the handle. Luckily I wasn't the one called on to answer him. Who knows what I would have said, but it certainly wouldn't have been calm and measured like Namuri's words. "Do you understand me, Peltron?" she went on sternly. "I need to hear you give your word before we free you and you can leave. You need to say it before all your men so they will hear you clearly and remember. Do you give your word that you will bring back our women to us unharmed and do no further damage here?"

His voice thick with anger, he answered, "I give my word that I will come here unarmed and bring back your women. In return I can take my son home. Now untie me so we can leave."

While Peltron and his men were finding their horses and making ready to leave, Adana clambered back up to the top of Hawk Mound. As he rode out through the gap with his men straggling after him, she stepped up again to her perch on the highest rock. In her frightening aspect, arms raised, little licks of falsefire rising once more from her hair, she shouted after him, "Peltron of Hernorium, if you ever think to come this way again to do harm, remember this day and rest assured that we will kill all of you next time. Tell that to your father the Magistrar as a message from the women of Nessian." Her voice, harsh with anger, echoed all through the grove. Peltron glanced back at her just once. Then, with a cry, he spurred his horse into a gallop, leaving the wagons to follow. Looking up at Adana, I felt a shiver of fear run up my back. It was as if she had turned herself into someone or rather something I didn't even know, something strange and terrible.

Watching all those men leave I wondered if the Magistrar had ordered this raid or if it had been Peltron's idea—either way a failure. I didn't envy him having to go home and explain to his father why men and horses had died in this raid that should have been so easily won. Altogether three horses had been killed by falling rocks and another three were so injured they had to be put down. Seven men were severely wounded, too hurt to ride home, and of those, two or three might not survive the trip back. Five men had died, three dead outright in the rockfall and another two at Peltron's hand because they were too damaged to mend. And now he would have to be the one to tell their families why their husband/brother/father/son would not be coming home from his little battle.

Not true. Actually Peltron owed no one an explanation, no one except the Magistrar. These men were his to do with as he pleased, just like the horses. Their lives were in his hands. If they all died because of his pride or stupidity he had only his father to answer to. He owned them, just as for that short time he had owned me and was free to give me to his brother, or rape me, or sell me to the slave pens with no one else to answer to—except perhaps Torvin. Ah yes, Torvin, what a peculiar bond we had. If I was to believe him he had come here to save my life, and now I owed him a strange debt of gratitude I couldn't possibly repay.

Even though I tried to prepare for the sight, it was still a shock to ride back into Nessian and see it as a charred and smoking ruin. We had won, if this disaster could be called winning. At least none of us had died, and now we had a hostage and because of that some hope of having our women returned to us. But what were we to do with Ramule in the meanwhile? In all this chaos there was no place for him. I had heard talk of dungeons and prison cells and such things from Banya when I was a prisoner myself in Hernorium, but we certainly had nothing like that here. We didn't even have a secure room since our houses had all been

103

damaged and were almost uninhabitable due to the effects of fire and water. We had brought him back tied to Wanuil's horse, and now we were standing about, many of us wet, all of us reeking of smoke and staggering with exhaustion, trying to decide what to do with our questionable prize.

Finally Morith said, "What about the festival pole? We could tie him there." She was speaking of the tall stout pole at the center of our public space where we hung banners for our different festivals—the sign of the turtle, the sign of the hawk or owl or snake—according to the season. That pole at least had not burned, as so much made of the wood in Nessian had.

"Not with a rope," I said quickly. "It won't work. He'll get himself free in no time." I knew enough about captives to know that. Then Namuri remembered that we had a long chain somewhere among all the metal trash in the barn, a chain with two padlocks and a key that she said some traders had left with us. We had never found any use for it, and most of us didn't even know it was there. Huldra quickly ran to fetch it and with it we chained our hostage to the pole. Luckily the chain was long enough to allow him some room to sit, lie down, even pace a little.

Nadir was shocked when she saw what we meant to do. She said indignantly, "You wouldn't treat a dog that way, keep it chained up like that."

"Quite right," Namuri said curtly. "We would never treat a dog that way, but Ramule is a man and men are a lot cleverer and more dangerous than dogs. Do you see a good, secure, comfortable, dry place where we can keep him? We have no roofs over any of our houses, much less a dry comfortable little cell we can secure."

"You said you would treat him fairly."

"And so we shall, but we can't give him what we ourselves don't have, what his father's men have destroyed. What would you have us do, Nadir, let him loose so he can go rejoin his father? The lives of our women depend on our keeping him here securely. We are using him to get back your friends. Otherwise we would gladly have sent him off with the others."

"Just ask him to give his word of honor that he won't run off," Nadir said as if this was actually a reasonable possibility. At that Wanuil gave a harsh laugh and made a rude comment about how much horse dung his word of honor might be worth. Then Nadir turned to me to make her appeal. "Solene, you know what it's like to be a captive. How can you see him treated this way?"

Ramule, I saw, was keeping his silence. Eyes cast down and face sullen, he was awaiting his fate at our hands. I shrugged and turned away. Yes, of course I knew what it was like to be a captive. And I also knew a captive was without "honor." I would have given my word, said anything, promised anything, told any lie—and all with no guilt—if it would have won me my freedom. And indeed I did just that, endangering two young women who never did me anything but kindness, but who stood between me and escape.

"Not good enough, Nadir, nothing we can trust," Namuri said firmly, shaking her head. "Now someone get the boy a dry mat if there's one to be found anywhere."

And so, before we could look to ourselves, we had to make temporary shelter for our captive, who muttered and grumbled ungratefully, watching everything we did with angry, frightened eyes. A mat was found, wet only on one corner, some dry covers and a lumpy pillow. We made a rough shelter of sorts by fastening several poles to the main pole and covering them with oiled canvas for some privacy, and as protection from dew and against rain if it should ever come in this dry season. We even brought him a little food, though we hardly had anything to eat ourselves that wasn't fire damaged.

Just as we were all about to leave, Namuri spotted Marn in the crowd. Clearly she didn't recognize her and her face went hard with anger. "Who are you and what are you doing here? If you're with those men and have come to do harm I swear I'll have you killed on the spot!" An astonishing speech for our usually kind and gentle Headwoman.

"Namuri, don't you recognize me? Don't you know who I am?"

Namuri's eyes went wide with surprise, but there was no

welcome in her voice. "Marn, is that really you? Why have you come back at this moment? Do you have anything to do with what happened here?"

"Nothing, I swear. I'm as shocked as any of you and wish I had been here to help against those men. I came home because I was lonely in the city. I missed Nessian—and most of all I missed Elani."

"Home? You dare to call this home with the way you left? The pain and misery you left behind you? Seven years gone! What makes you think Elani would want you back?" Namuri had good reason to dislike Marn. She had been witness to Elani's painful bouts of grief when Marn went away so suddenly and without explanation. Even before that, Marn with her harsh-sounding speech and her rough town ways had not been one of Namuri's favorite people. For all of Namuri's kindness and fairness, she was not one to welcome outsiders to come live among us.

Marn was nodding, looking solemn. "Yes, I always thought of it as home. It was the first real home I ever had and I always wanted to come back. I grieve for the pain I caused, but I had my own reasons for leaving that I won't speak of here. But if all of you don't want me here then I'll leave again. This time I won't be back. You'll never see my face again."

At that Elani stepped in front of Marn as if to protect her, though Elani was short and Marn was a good head taller. She threw up her hands and shouted, "Marn's back home and I want her here. This is the woman I love. It's my fault she left. I let my mother mistreat her and did nothing to stop it. If you can't welcome her back, if you send her away, I'll leave with her, I swear I will!"

I was astounded to hear Elani speak that way. She never raised her voice to anyone, much less to Namuri whom she revered.

With Elani's words Namuri said quickly, "No need for threats, Elani. Welcome home, Marn. Your skills are much needed here. You've come back at a terrible moment, but just in time to help us recover from this attack."

Then, as Namuri gave a quick nod and slipped away into the

crowd, Elani took Marn's hand and said in a voice tremulous with love, "Come home with me, Marn. I need you there." Strange words. What kind of home were they going to? What was even left of our house? Seeing them walk away together I wanted to cry for them—and for all of us.

Finally free to take care of our own needs, the rest of us went off to inspect the damage to our houses and try to find dry clothes, all except Nadir who stayed for a while to talk to Ramule and keep him company.

For the next few days, everything in Nessian was in chaos. We were like ants at the site of an overturned anthill, rushing about this way and that, trying frantically to repair the damage to our lives. The first day or so wet clothes and bedding were hanging everywhere, colorfully decorating the whole settlement as if for some bizarre festival or celebration. We found ourselves praying for the summer drought to continue, instead of praying for rain as we usually did at this time of year. If we thought we had worked hard before the raid, now we had to work twice as hard, but without the comfort of dry beds or home-cooked food or our own familiar houses to retreat to. Namuri's skills as Headwoman were stretched to the breaking point, even with Josian and Morith and Yora to help with the organizing. There were plenty of grumblings and complaints about all we had to do, but most of the time someone would end by saying, "Evandaru be praised that at least none of us died in the raid." Personally I would have been more grateful to Her if none of those men had come here in the first place. Besides the statement wasn't altogether true, but we didn't know that until later.

The second day Rialin and Fedra rode off to take the news of what had happened to the women hiding in the hills, telling them that we were all safe, but that the settlement had been torched and they couldn't all come back at once since there was no place for them yet. Two of those women returned with a wagon full of foodstuffs and pots and pans that had been hidden away and that were desperately needed now. They also brought the sad news that three of our oldest women had died from the hardship of being moved, Senli's great-grandmother among them. So now, added to all our other troubles was this terrible grief, especially heavy for Namuri.

As soon as the supply wagon was emptied, it was taken to the grove to be filled with weapons and armor. They would be stored in the loft of the big barn, at least until we could decide what to do with them all. More arguments ensued about whether we should destroy the lot or keep it for future use or barter it with the traders.

Women from the neighboring settlements and even from "Outside" began pouring in—to help us rebuild, to bring us supplies, kindness, love, whatever was needed. All this was much appreciated, but it also meant there were many new ones to guide and watch over and supervise and feed and even find places to sleep when we ourselves had no place. The big barn that had a slate roof and was our only undamaged building again became a dormitory. The barn floor was soon covered with bodies and our settlement was suddenly full of strange voices. Men also came, mostly traders we had dealt with before. They did not stay, but brought us much needed things such as dry food and warm blankets and clean clothes and footwear.

Those first nights we made a common fire and cooked big pots of soup or stew, some of it from the winter stores we had buried or root vegetables we dug too soon, because so much of our fresh garden food had been trampled. Besides, there was no way of cooking in any of our houses, damaged as they were. The work was hard and constant. Crews went into the forest to cut poles for rafters and logs for the mother-beams that had burned. All that wood then had to be peeled and shaped. Other crews went to the swamp below the river bend to cut rushes for re-thatching the roofs, rushes that then had to be bundled and made ready. The only still thing in this constant, exhausting activity was Ramule, who watched it all with a look of sullen disdain from the chair we had brought for him. Except for Nadir, none of us bothered trying to speak to him. He was too surly and angry.

There was no reward in it. And besides we were far too busy.

Marn tried to be everywhere at once, wanting to help Elani rebuild and at the same time wanting to re-establish her place in the settlement and help with everything else. She seemed to be running herself to exhaustion—but then I suppose we all were.

With Marn directing, the five of us—myself, Karil, Elani, Marn and Adana—had been struggling to clear our house of burned-through rafters that had fallen inside and were blocking access to the rooms. We needed to see if the mother-beam was still sound enough to support a new roof. Partway through, Marn said it was time to stop and rest. All of us were filthy, exhausted, frustrated and coated with wet soot. I offered to go fetch us a large bowl of hot soup from the common fire.

On the way back, as I passed our hostage, Ramule called out to me to complain of the food, saying it was "not fit for dogs." I felt such a surge of fury I might have hit him if my hands hadn't been full at that moment and so broken our pledge.

"I know this isn't the fine Palace food you're accustomed to," I told him with angry sarcasm. "But you're eating just what we're all eating because our crops have been destroyed by Peltron's men riding through our gardens. Don't you see what your father has done here? Besides, this food is a lot better than the scraps I was fed as a captive on the road."

Ramule turned his face away and fell back into sullen silence, but Nadir, who had been sitting by him, said quickly, "He's not responsible for what his father did." I shook my head and rushed home with our soup, needing to be away from there before I did something rash.

My time in Hernorium had certainly not made me kind and merciful, quite the opposite. It was a good thing we had made our pledge, given our word. Otherwise I might well have been tempted to hurt this young man for what his father had done. I was too busy and too angry and gave no thought to the fact that Ramule was little more than a boy himself and might feel lonely and frightened and helpless among all these hostile strangers, in an unfamiliar place so far from home. Also, he had good reason to fear us. If his father didn't return as promised, he might well die at our hands. That was what we had pledged to do.

Still I had no patience for him and never once thought that his sullen anger might only be his way of protecting himself in such harsh circumstances, the little scrap of armor he had left to cover his pride. I got back with our soup so angry my hands were shaking and found everyone else in a joyful mood. The mother-beam was sound. Though scorched in many places, it was still strong enough to hold up our new roof.

Over the next week or so, our old women and children and possessions gradually began drifting back, a wagonload at a time. It wasn't easy finding decent space for them, but it was also too hard to keep the camp in the hills going with any degree of comfort or safety. And so, on top of all our other burdens, we had to deal, as gently as we could, with their bewilderment and grief at seeing their homes and their settlement in ruins.

For a while our girls turned into wild things. Since the adults in their lives were much too busy to adequately care for them, they turned to each other and formed little packs that marauded around the settlement, dashing about helping or hindering us in our work, raiding the food stash or disappearing altogether on adventures of their own and worrying us all. The raid had breached their sense of safety. They had learned to rely on each other in the camp and they put more trust in each other than in the adults who had been powerless to stop this terrible thing from happening.

Ishta, Garnith's granddaughter, was the leader of one such pack, by far the most troublesome and destructive. No amount of scolding or threats had any effect on her, not even from Namuri. Ishta was like a runaway horse, rushing heedlessly on her own way. Finally Garnith solved the problem by tying her up next to Ramule. "You're more trouble than Peltron and all his men put together. Sit here and make yourself useful learning whatever Nadir is teaching Ramule."

Shandi, Ishta's mother, objected, saying, "I won't have my

daughter treated like one of those raiders."

Garnith just shrugged and said, "Well, she's acting like one of those raiders. If you have a better solution, Daughter, do it. Otherwise let her be. It won't do her any harm and she may even learn something useful."

Seeing Ishta tied up like that had a sobering effect on the wildest of the girls and they gave us less trouble after that. When I passed by I was surprised to see that Ramule seemed to have taken an interest in the girl and in showing her how to make things. Or perhaps it was Ishta who had taken an interest in Ramule. He was certainly the strangest and most interesting thing to land in her world. A few times I stopped in some inconspicuous spot to watch them together, thinking that perhaps Ramule was not so bad after all if he could befriend a child that way. Maybe they were taming each other. Even after Ishta was untied she continued to stay by Ramule whenever possible, sometimes even sitting on his knee. Seeing this didn't make me start to like him, but I didn't hate him quite so much.

Much like Marn, I threw myself into the repairs, rushing from one site to the other, trying to get everything done and exhausting myself in the process. I suppose I still felt some guilt for the raid as if it was somehow my fault that these men had come here, though Namuri and my mother and whoever else I spoke to assured me that it wasn't so. I think I was also trying to avoid seeing how distant Adana and I had become and how close she was to Karil.

With Marn back, Adana had moved into one of the canvas shelters set up in a field where many other young women were staying. She was certainly not moving back in with her mother since she had moved into our house to escape her. Adana said it was to give us space, but in fact I thought she wanted space herself. I had hardly seen her since the battle. The third or fourth day afterward, she came to look for me where I was working up a ladder fastening a pole in place.

"We need to talk, Solene, and we always seem to be too tired at night for serious words." I came down, not sorry to stop work since my back and arms were aching, but very much afraid of what she might say. We went together and sat under a tree.

"When all this repairing is over and our women are safely home, I'm going to move to a city. I don't suppose you want to come with me."

This was a sort of non-invitation, but I understood that I still had a choice and now it was up to me. In reality I had no choice. The very thought of going to a city made my skin crawl and set my stomach to roiling with nausea. I shook my head. "No, I don't. I wish I did but I can't."

"You know, Solene, not all cities are like Hernorium."

She was holding out a branch to me, but I couldn't take it. I knew I was making the final choice and I knew what that would mean between us, but still I shook my head. The very thought was terrifying. I shuddered.

"If you're very sure, then I might take your suggestion and ask your sister Karil."

I felt grief burn my eyes, but I shrugged and said in as calm a voice as I could manage, "That would probably be a good thing for both of you. She certainly isn't very happy here." I had thought that Marn's return would make Karil happy. She had always said Marn was her real mother. Instead she appeared to be jealous of both our mothers. They did indeed seem very wrapped up in each other.

All my hard work didn't stop me in the days that followed from seeing how far apart Adana and I had drifted, like a road that divides and goes two separate ways. Eventually one day she came over to me at the cook-fire circle. "It's been decided, Solene. Karil and I are going to the city together. It's better that way. We have more in common." I wondered what would have happened if I told her at that moment that I had changed my mind and would go with her after all.

"Do you love her?" I had to ask though I dreaded the answer.

"I'm learning to."

"What a strange answer. No wonder Karil wasn't anxious to

112

have me back."

"Karil was very worried about you."

"Well, she may have worried," I shot back angrily, "but she certainly wasn't glad to see me back."

Adana shook her head, looking sad. "You see how quickly we quarrel. We need only say a few words to each other and we're at odds."

And Karil is the cause of it all, I wanted to say, but of course I knew that wasn't the truth. Adana and I had had this quarrel going long before Karil had become an intimate part of her life, when Karil was still just my younger sister. "Go then with my love," I said with rough grief in my voice. "It's better so. You'll be happy there. Surely you're not happy here. And there's no way I could go with you, especially now, not after everything that's happened." I knew I sounded angry. In truth all I wanted to do was cry. So much lost. At least it had not been any of our lives, not in the raid itself. How wise of Josian to get us all out of harm's way.

While we were waiting for food from the big pot, I saw Karil glowering at me, as if I stood between her and her heart's desire. I beckoned her over and she came resentfully, dragging her feet, making dust cloud up around her. Echoing the words Josian had said the morning after she brought me home, I said, "I am not your enemy, Karil. Adana and I have separated. There is no way we can build a life together. This is my home and I'm not leaving here, at least not for a long time. She needs the life and excitement of a city. As far as I'm concerned you're welcome to go there with her and share her life. I promise you I'm not standing in your way. It's Adana you have to convince, not me. You need to woo her, not threaten me."

After that I saw them together more and more, and I would catch Karil giving me little sideways gloating looks, as if she had finally won the prize in the contest and I was the loser.

I would miss Adana but not Karil, not for a long time, not until she went away somewhere else and grew up a little. After all, Adana and I had been friends since childhood, long before we became lovers. Of course Karil and I had been sisters all our lives, but I don't think we were ever friends. The poison of jealousy had always been there, at least on her side, making me the enemy, no matter how hard I tried to win her over and make up for her hurt. I didn't find her smug little looks of triumph endearing, just the opposite. Ah well, she finally had what she had wanted for so long. I trust it gave her joy. It didn't seem to make her kind.

"Do you treat all of your prisoners this way?" Ramule called out to me. He was sitting at a table Nadir had set up for him, working with Nadir and some of the other women from Hamlin, making bundles of the newly picked reeds so they could be used for thatching our roofs. It was Nadir who had taught him, saying, "He has to have something useful to do or he'll go mad chained up that way." None of the rest of us had bothered.

At first he had been clumsy with the work. He had never worked with his hands before, and it seemed to me more trouble than it was worth to try teaching him, but Namuri thought it would be good for him to understand what had been destroyed so quickly by his own people and the sort of effort with which it had been made. Then Nadir volunteered to undertake his education and worked patiently next to him day after day, teaching him to bundle thatch. She had fashioned a rough plank tabletop, set up on log ends and with benches to match, next to where he was tied. Then she fastened a sort of sunshade over it all and taught him the skill.

I had just spent a hot, sweaty, exhausting day, snaking poles out of the forest with the help of horses and ropes. I had fallen several times and was bruised, cut, sore and very out of sorts. I certainly had no patience with Ramule at that moment. Head down with weariness, I had even forgotten about him as I passed him on my way home.

Now I whirled around to face him, annoyed at having been accosted in that way. "Prisoners? What do you mean prisoners? We know nothing of prisoners. You're the only one, the only one we have ever had and hopefully the only one we will ever have. We have no jails or dungeons here such as you have in Hernorium. If we have disagreements here, we settle them among ourselves. If someone gives us too much trouble we send them away to live elsewhere, hoping they'll do better there. Sometimes they come back when they've had enough time to heal. Sometimes they make a new life somewhere else. No matter, we do not keep prisoners. And we will be only too glad to send you home when you've been exchanged for our own women that your father stole away from us.

"I'm glad to see they've put you to useful work so you can mend a little of what that man destroyed. You came here with your father and his men to do harm. Why do you think you're entitled to be treated kindly?"

His eyes flashed at me and his nostrils flared. At that moment he looked very angry and very much like Peltron. "Do you really think I wanted to come here? What for? My father made me. I argued, he insisted, even threatened. My mother didn't want me to come. When she cried, he hit her. He said if I was going to be Magistrar, there were things I needed to learn. Why ever would I want to leave the city where I was comfortable and happy and come to this wild desolate place that's been nothing but misery for me?"

"Do you know that he wanted to capture us and make us slaves and kill all those that didn't suit him?"

"He didn't really share his plans with me, only that he wanted to recapture you."

"And you think it's right for some people to be slaves, to lose all their freedom and their rights to others?"

"I suppose I never thought that much about it. There were always slaves in the Palace when I was growing up. No one ever said it was wrong, not even my mother." He spoke in a burst of honesty that made me give him another look.

"You see," Nadir said. "No use hating him. He was just a boy doing his father's bidding. How could he have refused?"

I shook my head, wondering, *Just how old does someone have to be before we have a right to hold them responsible for what they do to us,*

115

the right to hate them? Was Peltron perhaps just a more grown-up boy doing his father's bidding or trying to find favor there? Where did it stop, this chain of grief and pain and cruelty? Who was to blame? When men come to kill or enslave you are you just supposed to say, not their fault? Their fathers made them do it? Where does it all end? And then I remembered that we ourselves had killed, not intentionally of course, but nonetheless those men were dead at our hands.

I sighed. Looking more closely at Ramule now, I saw him perhaps for the first time as just his own self, not as Peltron's son or the Magistrar's grandson or a part of Hernorium. He was just a young man of wealth, growing up sheltered and privileged, with as little knowledge of the world as I had, maybe less, and now living in terrible circumstances that he could never have imagined. His father had wanted to bring him on this trip to harden him, to make a man of him in his own model. Perhaps Peltron had made a very grave error exposing his son to another world.

Watching his busy hands, moving all the time we spoke, I nodded at him. "You're doing good work with those rushes. It's not easy to keep the bundles even. Nadir must be a very patient teacher. It takes skilled hands to make those knots." It was a struggle to say those words. I felt awkward. They came out stiff and stilted. Nonetheless, as I turned to walk away, I saw him flush with pleasure, and my heart was just a little less hardened with anger.

Then, before I could soften too much he said rudely, "If you would just set me free and not keep me chained like an animal I could do real work, a man's work with tools, not sit here all day with a bunch of women."

"Not well spoken, Ramule," Nadir scolded, but she didn't sound too upset.

I turned back with a hand raised as if to strike. "This is much better than you deserve," I growled at him.

Nadir grabbed my wrist and shook her head. "Can't you see how much he's hurting? How would you like to be chained here, helpless, for everyone to stare at with anger? It's only out of pain he speaks that way. Don't you have any kindness in your heart, Solene?"

"No, not anymore," I said bitterly. Then I leaned down and said in Nadir's ear. "Peltron killed it when he raped me and then beat me so I couldn't walk." I said this just to her, and not in front of Ramule, so I must have had some kindness in me after all. I had to admit, Nadir had seen something in Ramule that I certainly hadn't. Perhaps it was love that had transformed him in her eyes, but then again love only comes when your heart is open.

At first I wasn't that glad to have Marn back. She hardly spoke to me at all. In fact she seemed to avoid me when she could. She seemed like a stranger—cold, hard, distant—almost like those men at the dogfights, not like a real woman, at least not like one of our women. I couldn't find the person there that I used to love and had missed so desperately when she left. I actually resented this shadow semblance who had come back in her place, but she treated my mother with reverence and tenderness, and my mother responded like a flower opening to the sun. For that, at least, I had to love Marn and be grateful.

After a while I realized Marn was just shy with us, uncomfortable, afraid we would push her away in anger for having left us the way she did. Also she didn't know how to talk to us over that chasm of seven lost years. When she left we were children and now we were young women. Finally I understood that it was up to me. I knew Marn could never be my mother again. It was too late for that now, that time was long over. But maybe she could be my friend if I would allow it.

It seemed the best way to forge a connection with Marn was to go and work next to her. When I did that she began to talk to me about the city and about her life there, tentatively at first and then with animation when she saw I was really interested. And she also started to tell me stories from her past, stories that were full of wit and bitter humor and an outsider's view of human actions. As the days went by we did indeed become friends of a sort, establishing a new and different kind of bond and losing most of our shyness with each other. She also taught me some of the things she had learned in the outside world.

Once we renewed our connection I realized how good it was to have Marn back. Our home felt complete again. And it was wonderful to see my mother happy. She had been right to wait. She knew something we didn't when we urged her to forget and find someone else. For her the call of the heart ran very deep.

Marn and I were putting up some boards to side a shed when I gathered the courage to ask, "Was it because of Grandmother Orlin that you left?"

"I left because I almost hit your mother, had a hand raised to strike her. Elani of all people, the kindest, gentlest person I ever knew! My anger and frustration were breaking through, getting beyond my control. I knew it was only a matter of time before it actually happened. That's when I left, when I saw my hand raised to her in that way and I knew it would happen the next time or the time after that.

"But yes, it was because of Orlin. A curse on that old woman! She was the cause of all our troubles. Aside from her, your mother and I never quarreled about anything. Orlin made a horror of our lives those last few years. She died soon after I left. Bless that snake; I could make a shrine to it even now. But I was already living in the city of Rockhill and didn't even know she was dead, not for three years, not until I heard it from some trading man who had passed through here on his travels. By then I had the habit of living in the city and living alone. I was afraid to come back. Actually I thought Elani was better off without me and would soon find someone else.

"You were three when I first met your mother. The sight of her caught my eye. I followed her home from the market in Hamlin. In the beginning I think Orlin even welcomed me. She had despaired of Elani ever being with anyone, she was so shy and quiet. Less than a year later we got Karil. Gradually I let my heart open. The three of you became my family for a while, something I had never had before.

"I must say, your grandmother was never an easy person.

Other people didn't like her. Even her three sisters, your great-aunts, avoided her and your cousins wanted nothing to do with her. But I knew how to manage—or thought I did. I charmed her and flattered her and even teased her about her ways. For a while we had a truce of sorts. I would have done anything to be with your mother. She was like the sun, pouring light into my day. No one had ever loved me that way before. I was a child of the streets. At that time you and your sister and your mother were my whole life.

"Orlin wasn't so bad during those early years. I flattered myself that I had tamed her meanness, that she wouldn't treat me that way. Then, as she got older she got worse, more quarrelsome, bitter, angry, bossy, more difficult—no, not difficult, she was always difficult—impossible. When she got sick, she turned into a terrible tyrant. I hated to see the way she treated your mother. She had Elani in tears more often than not. After she got well it was as if her body had recovered but not her mind. If I stayed I might easily have hit the old woman, and that would have been even worse.

"It was your grandmother's house then. After her illness was over, I kept asking Elani to move, to take the two of you and go away with me, begging really, but she kept saying, 'My mother's not doing well. She still needs me. How can I leave her? Who will care for her if I go?' Good question indeed! Who would? She had no other children and the rest of her family wanted nothing to do with her, especially as she got worse. Clearly there was no one else interested in getting involved in that thankless work.

"That's what we fought about. Your grandmother had a terrible hold on Elani and she was like poison for the rest of us. Interesting that she died of poison. When I left I couldn't even say goodbye to the three of you because if I had I would have begged your mother one more time to go and that would only have led to another fight."

"I don't think Karil has forgiven you yet for leaving."

"Ah, Karil, I'm sad about her but what can I do? She never forgives and she never forgets. I don't think she has ever forgiven anyone for anything. She's probably never forgiven her first mother for abandoning her. Personally I didn't really think we needed a second child. As you know, your mother seldom asks for anything, but when she does she can be very persuasive and she's likely to get her way. She wanted that child, fell in love with her the minute she saw her and had to bring her home. But no matter how much love Elani poured out on Karil it didn't return to her, only jealousy and the need for more. Karil has Adana now and perhaps that will make her happy."

"Especially if she thinks she's taken her away from me," I said with some bitterness.

"You have to let go of that, Solene. You don't want to end up like your grandmother, do you? How can new love find room in your life if you're all full of bitterness?"

I was about to make an angry retort when I realized she had spoken out of love. Maybe Marn had a little mothering left in her after all. I turned and gave her a long thoughtful look. "Marn, I understand why you left the way you did and I'm very glad you came back. I don't want to say I forgive you because that would imply there was something to forgive and I had the right to give or withhold my forgiveness. Let me just say it's really good to have you home again."

Sixteen days! Rialin, one of our scouts, rode in all excited to tell us that Peltron was on his way back and that he had a wagon with him. "They must have turned around and come right back as soon as they had gathered our women," Namuri said. "Peltron must have been very anxious for the return of his son or perhaps his wife gave him a great deal of grief for taking the boy with him on such a foolish venture—and worse grief for leaving him here. Even the most subservient wife can become a fiercely protective mother when her children are endangered." I pictured Monice really angry and realized I wouldn't want to get crosswise with her in such a mood.

When the men were half a day's ride away, Fedra rode home to alert us. Morith and Wanuil and several others rode out to escort them in. Meanwhile, reluctantly, we all strapped on our homemade swords again. Though they were awkward to wear, we wanted to be ready for any eventuality. After all, we had no reason to trust these men. There had been a heated meeting and argument about whether to bring them to the grove or to the settlement. Finally it was solved when Adana said, "We should meet with them here. That way we can keep the boy chained where he is and not have to drag him out there, both an inconvenience and a danger."

As soon as we heard the sound of horses coming, the whole settlement poured out into the streets from our houses and gardens, cheering and shouting welcomes. Led and flanked by our riders, Peltron and his men rode in single file. They were followed by a wagon driven by Torvin with four women in it, our three being returned and Dorial with them. Peltron was glowering, but Torvin seemed to be laughing at something one of the women had said to him. In contrast to his brother's scowling face he looked almost joyous. Before the wagon had come to a full stop our women were out of it. They were quickly swallowed up in the arms of their families and disappeared with them. I went to greet Dorial, but she had vanished with the others, Valdru's family I think. They must have become friends on the journey home. I called out anxiously to Torvin, "Banya? Where is Banya?"

"She didn't want to come. Her grandmother is very ill. I gave her some money and sent her home to be with the old woman until she recovered or died." *How like Torvin*, I thought, glad Banya had been taken care of.

Meanwhile Peltron was shouting, "Where is Ramule? Where is my son? What have you done with him? Why isn't he here to greet me?" He sounded almost as frightened as he did angry.

Ramule called out, "I'm right here, Father. I'm fine. Nothing to worry about."

Peltron swung about at the sound of Ramule's voice and I saw a look of shock on his face. "What! Chained to a post! Tied up like a dog! Is this how you women keep your promises? At much trouble and expense I brought back your girls, even an extra one. Why isn't my son free?"

Namuri came up to him holding out the key. "I'm going to free him right now. We weren't sure we could trust you. We had to have our women safely home before we could let him go."

"Then hurry up, old woman. Every minute he's chained is an outrage, every second...!"

At those words of disrespect for our Headwoman there was an angry muttering and even some flashing of swords. I found myself with an itchy hand on my hilt. I had to think Peltron either very brave or very foolish to speak that way when surrounded and vastly outnumbered by armed women. Namuri was hurrying over to the pole as fast as her cane and lame foot would allow, but I was afraid something might happen, some burst of temper or rashness from among us that would cause an eruption of violence. After all, those of us carrying swords knew how to use them now and we had no reason to love these men. Just as the angry voices were rising to a dangerous level I heard Ramule shout, "I'm not going back with you, Father."

At almost the same moment Peltron and Namuri shouted back at him, "What do you mean, not going back?"

Namuri stopped partway, looking back and forth in bewilderment between father and son. "But you have to go back, Ramule. That was the agreement, the promise we made. We are pledged to turn you over to your father in exchange for our women."

At the same moment Peltron roared, "Of course you're going back with me. I've come all this way to fetch you and given up three slaves as ransom and had to pay a good sum of money for their release. What have they done to you? Have they tortured you? Twisted your mind? Forced you to say this?"

Looking from one to the other, Ramule said calmly, "Namuri, let's say that you've honorably made the trade and it's done. I'm still not going back. Father, no one forced or harmed me. I was well treated. If you and I went off to speak in private I would say the same thing. Besides I've been free for a while now. Nadir knew where the key was kept. She unfastened the padlocks this morning, saying I should be free to make my own choices. Look!" As he spoke he unwound the chain from the post. Then he held it high in both hands for us all to see. "In the confusion, no one thought to check it. I could have left anytime, but I gave her my word of honor that I would stay and I'm still here. So you can see, Father, I'm not being held against my will."

Everyone had gone silent. We all turned to stare at him in amazement. He was standing there grinning, full of his own power, almost beautiful, holding up his chain with the dangling padlocks, defying us all with a kind of shining innocence.

After a moment or so of silence Peltron said forcefully, "You still have to come with me." Under his gruff tone I could sense a sort of bewildered uncertainty.

"Not unless you want to bring me home in chains. Otherwise I'm going west with Nadir to see more of the world." At those words Nadir came up and put her arm around Ramule's waist, smiling up at him and then turning a look of proud defiance on the rest of us.

Torvin had tied the wagon horses to a tree. He now walked over to stand next to his brother. He was trying to get Peltron's attention, but Peltron seemed intent on ignoring him. He had eyes only for Ramule. "Enough of this nonsense, Ramule. Get on your horse so we can leave this place."

"I'm not going."

"Of course you are! As your father I command you to! Now!" When Ramule shook his head, Peltron shouted to his men, "Seize him! Bring him here to me!" The men shifted uneasily, leaning forward as if they wanted to obey yet were afraid. After all, their previous encounter with us had been far from pleasant. At that same moment Torvin raised both hands and roared in a voice of command such as I had never heard him use before, "Don't move, any of you! Stay on your horses! Don't think to touch him!" Meanwhile several women moved in the way, getting between Ramule and his father's men.

"What kind of man are you?" Peltron yelled at his son in

frustration. "Are you going to hide behind women?"

"If I have to, if you're going to call in your men to enforce your will and drag me away."

Peltron turned on Torvin. "Why are you interfering this way, you fool? He's my son, not yours." He started to urge his horse forward, but Torvin grabbed the bridle to stop him. "Brother, he's not yours to command anymore. That time is over now."

Then Namuri stepped forward and said firmly, "Peltron, we can't allow you to take him. He's declared his will. He's free, just like any of us."

"You've made him a hostage again. How do I know it's really of his own free will?"

"Father, I've already told you, even if I ride away with you and speak privately in your ear it will still be the same thing. I want to stay. Don't make this any harder. Tell my mother I love her and that I'll be back when I'm done with wandering."

Peltron's tone changed. I thought I could even hear some sadness in it. "But she's already picked out a bride for you."

"Then tell her to let the girl go. When the time comes I'll pick out my own bride." Then, with an abrupt change of tone he asked, "Father, why did you order this settlement burned?"

Peltron shrugged as if this was no big thing. "When you mount a raid that's what you do. You burn their houses. That lessens resistance."

Ramule opened his mouth as if he was going to answer, maybe even argue. Then he shut it again, and his whole face closed down. He gave his father a look that was not a boy's look, a hard look that would have made me tremble if it had been aimed at me.

Meanwhile Namuri was banging hard on the ground with her cane. "That's enough now. It's time to move on, Peltron, and take your men with you. Let us be. You've intruded enough on our lives already, done enough damage here."

Peltron whirled on her, furious. "How do I know he's safe here?"

"Your son is in our world now and we'll guard his welfare

as best we can. No one here means him harm." She answered calmly enough, but I could see her hand on the cane was shaking and her eyes were glittering with anger.

"Do you guarantee his safety?"

At that I stepped forward, wanting to face this man directly, needing to master my fear and hatred of him. "Of course not," I said, looking him right in the eye. "It's a dangerous world out there, as I've discovered to my grief. We can't guarantee anybody's safety, not even yours, not even our own. We can only guarantee our intentions toward him, which will always be good. On that much we can give you our word." I was amazed to hear myself saying these words and even more amazed to realize I meant them. Then I gave Peltron a long hard look, "Though, of course, if you return with armed men then none of us are safe here, not even the grandson of the Magistrar of Hernorium."

"Is that a threat?"

"A threat, a warning or a fact—take it however you wish, Peltron. To put it simply, do not come back here to do harm. It will cause you more pain than it's worth." I stared into his eyes until he finally looked away and turned his attention on his son again.

"Ramule, you're a fool and you're making the mistake of your life, but you'll have to live with it. You're not my son anymore. I disown you. Don't think to come home begging for your favored place in the Palace."

With that Peltron shifted his anger to his brother standing next to him, lashing out in frustration, "All your fault, Torvin, all of it, everything that's happened. If you could only have found yourself a woman that pleased you in Hernorium Father would have been satisfied, those men would not have died, Ramule would be safe at home and we would not be here in this hateful place. All this because you're a selfish fool."

"Brother, I never asked you to..."

Peltron interrupted with a rush of words as if Torvin wasn't even speaking. "There's been talk. I didn't believe it before, but maybe it's true. There are those who say perhaps the reason you could never find a woman to please you was because you really prefer men in that way, that you are really a Santeel." He spoke this last part with scathing contempt, every word full of malice, especially the final one. Clearly he wanted to goad Torvin into an angry response.

Seeing the look of alarm on the faces of the other men, I took a step back. I suppose such words would have meant a bloody fight in Hernorium. All of us fell into a tense silence, looking warily from one brother to the other, expecting some sort of violence to break out any moment.

Torvin stared up at Peltron for a long time without saying a word, but instead of looking angry he looked thoughtful. It seemed as if many things were passing through his mind at once. Finally, with a look of wonder on his face, he said, "A Santeel, eh? Now there's a thought. Who knows, Brother, you may well be right. That would explain many things, wouldn't it? Why I liked women, respected them, treated them as my equals, but could never fall in love with any of them no matter how attractive I found them. Nor could I ever feel myself burning with desire even when I most wanted to. Solene came the closest, but even with her it never quite happened." He shook his head. "Something to think on, I suppose. Yes, you may well be right."

Peltron was clearly taken by surprise. He actually looked shocked. I suppose he had expected a burst of anger and a heated denial. Shaking his head in disbelief, he growled, "You don't mean that. You're only trying to anger me more, as if things weren't already bad enough." With that he turned away, shouting at his men to make ready to leave, sending some of them for the wagon. Torvin watched impassively, showing no signs of departure. At last Peltron said in a calmer tone, "Time to go home now, Brother. Get on your horse. We have returned the captives, and Ramule is safe—as best we can tell. Let's be gone quickly from this rotten place. We have a long ride ahead of us before we're safely home."

Torvin shook his head. He had a strange, sad look on his face. "I'm not going back either, Brother. There's no way I can go now.

126

I wouldn't be welcome there. If I'm really a Santeel, as you say, it would cost me my life to return to Hernorium."

"Don't be a fool. I didn't mean it. I spoke in anger. It will all be forgotten by tomorrow."

"No matter. It may also be that you spoke the truth, a truth I've kept from myself all these years. And no, it won't be forgotten, not even by your order. It's been heard and witnessed by all these men."

"I'll command my men not to repeat a word of it. I'll order them to forget everything they heard."

Torvin laughed but without much humor in it. "You overreach yourself, Peltron. Not even you have that kind of power, the power to quell gossip and silence memory. Now leave me my horse and go back to Hernorium. I can't go with you."

"You don't mean any of this. It's only an aberration of this place, the effect of these unnatural women. You'll get over it soon enough when you're back home. We'll find you a good woman. You can marry and have children and be happy."

"No, I don't think I'll get over it. And we already know I'll never find that 'good woman.' If that's really who I am, a Santeel, then I have a long journey of discovery in front of me. Anyhow, the Magistrar would hardly welcome home a Santeel son. And besides, I can't live in a place where dogs are trained to kill each other."

Shouting "Get ready to leave now!" Peltron raised his hand as if to strike Torvin. With a growl, Adana pushed her way between them. She raised her head high and broadened her shoulders to seem more formidable. I saw Peltron shrink back from her with a look of fear on his face. "Not here!" she boomed out in her terrible power voice. "You cannot do that here! Leave him! Go home in peace before we change our minds about letting you go at all."

Peltron lowered his hand and gave Torvin one last glance that was almost a plea. At that moment Peltron looked old and beaten, caught in a world he didn't understand and couldn't control. When Torvin shook his head again, Peltron summoned his men with a gesture, spun his horse around and started down the road, followed by the wagon, now empty of its human cargo. He was going home without his brother and without his son, probably the only two people in the world he loved. For just a moment I felt a touch of pity for this man I would gladly have killed such a short while ago.

Adana shouted after him, "Don't think to come back or send more men. Next time we will kill you all! Not one of you will be left alive." The harsh, grating anger in her voice sent shivers up my back.

Josian joined her and added, "Don't think to look this way again with greedy eyes. Next time all the West Country will rise against you, not just a few women's settlements, but all the Women's Enclave and the cities of the 'Outside' as well. And next time, as Adana says, we will kill you. Believe it! We could have killed you before, killed you all." Then she shrugged. "But it would have been too messy, so much death, so many bodies to deal with. Next time we won't be so fussy. Bother us again and you may find all of West Country at your gates, armed and angry."

Other women began shouting insults at their departing backs, and soon the separate words were lost in a rising torrent of furious sound. Trying to be heard over the noise, I leaned toward Josian and asked, "What do you think? Are they gone for good? Is it really over?"

She nodded, "I think so, at least for now. Good that we have Ramule as a willing hostage. That will make them think twice before they come after us again. But we can only fool them once with smoke and falsefire. Next time, if there is a next time, they'll be ready for our tricks, and we'll have to think up a much better defense. Only Evandaru knows for sure if this is the first battle of a whole new war or the last battle of a very old one."

I saw Torvin with his head bowed, looking lost and bewildered, almost frightened, standing silent in the midst of that crowd of shouting, cheering, jeering women who were cursing his departing brother. I came up quickly and put a hand on his arm. "It's my turn now to show you a place of beauty. Come with me to the river. It's peaceful there. There's too much noise and chaos here."

This time we were in my territory. Torvin found himself holding onto my arm for support.

"What have I just done?" he asked with a mix of fear and wonder in his voice, "What have I just done? I've declared myself a Santeel and I'm not even sure what that means. In just a few words, in less than a minute, I have altered my whole life and there's no turning back, no way to undo it. What am I to do now?"

"Stay with us for a while, be an uncle for Ramule, help with the rebuilding and then see what happens when..."

"But I have no skill for such things and no experience," he interrupted. There was real anguish in his voice as he held up his hands. They were pale and soft, very clean, no dirt under the nails, no calluses and no scars.

"You can learn. Come now, the river waits." I took his hand, and he made no more protest as we walked together down to the edge of the water. There we sat side by side on the mossy bank. Huge trees leaned over the river, their branches reaching out from either side, making a dappled green archway overhead. The water here flowed smooth and swift over the sandy bottom with hardly a ripple, a lovely blue-green color. Just beyond the bend there were rapids and we could hear the musical chatter of water over stones.

We were silent for a while, each of us sunk in thought, until finally Torvin said, "Strange how like my dream this is, the red-headed woman sitting next to me at the water's edge."

"Not the place," I said sharply, already troubled by my fondness for this man. "I know the place in your dream and this is not it."

Torvin went on as if oblivious to my tone, "It's all very beautiful here, but you have to understand, this is as strange and different for me as the city was for you."

I made a wide sweep with my hand that took in everything around us. "This is my true home. This is where I live more than in any house—this river, these woods."

"And to think that I wanted to marry you and to have you live with me in the Palace. You knew better, didn't you?"

"Marriage was never part of my plans, Torvin, not possible. I knew I was going to get free or die in the attempt. But hurting you made me sad."

"Not sad enough to stay."

"No, not sad enough to stay. I would have died there. Besides, look what happened. In the end, by leaving, I freed us both."

"Yes, thanks to you I've been freed. Make no mistake about it, I'm grateful to you, Solene, very grateful. But now the question is, freed for what? What am I supposed to do with this life that is suddenly mine to choose? I have no idea. It's all too new." He shook his head and for a while sat staring at the rushing water as if in a trance. Then he turned to look at me and said abruptly, "I suppose we should go back up to the others. They may be looking for you, wondering if you're safe here with the enemy. Will they hate me, all those women, for the destruction done here by my brother?"

"Maybe, some of them, but most of them will love you as my friend and because you're a good man. And you are my friend, aren't you, Torvin, even though I betrayed you by leaving?"

"I'll always be your friend, Solene. You only did what you needed to do." After that we walked up the hill together arm in arm.

That evening there was a celebration for the return of our women, a celebration with eating and music and singing and dancing around a blazing fire fed by the burnt remnants of our roofs and sheds. First the three captives told their stories of capture and return. Listening to their experiences, I painfully relived my own. Senli and Tarsel I didn't know very well, but Valdru was my cousin. We had been friends all our lives. My heart ached for all of them when I thought of what they had endured in that city and most especially for her. There was much angry muttering afterward about what we should have done to those men and that perhaps we had let them go much too easily.

Later we all ate together, not much of a feast due to the effects of the raid, but the best we could manage. The whole evening was a strange mix of joy and sorrow, grief for what had happened, joy for the safe return of our women. We started off the dancing with some big noisy circle dances to draw everyone in. When I saw Torvin hanging back with a sad, thoughtful look on his face, I snagged his arm and dragged him into the circle. Then I saw Dorial standing shyly to one side, watching hesitantly, and drew her in also.

Afterward the larger dance dissolved into couples dancing with each other and I had to suffer pangs of envy, watching Adana and Karil dancing together. They were looking adoringly into one another's faces or at least that's how it seemed to me. *What did you expect?* I asked myself. *You practically threw them together. You need to accept what is.* I was trying my best to do that, but when Adana finally asked me to dance, my hurt prevailed. I refused her, turned away and went instead to dance with others, including Torvin. In fact I danced with him several times. The third time I leaned over and whispered to him, "You see, we are dancing together at the ball after all." I was pleased to see him smile back at me with some real pleasure in his face. Just then Tarsel came up and said to me loudly enough for him to hear, "I see you dancing with that man. Don't think *I* plan to be his friend after what his brother's men did to me." Valdru came up beside her and said even louder, as if for everyone to hear, "Torvin was the one who came to free me and he was nothing but kindness on the way back. Not just to me but to all of us, even Dorial. He's not like his brother, or Solene would never have befriended him." The next moment both of them were swept away in the swirl of dancing. I looked at Torvin and shrugged. He gave me a rueful smile.

It was good to see that other women asked Torvin to dance, as he was certainly too shy in that scene to ask for himself. I was pleased to dance with Dorial and to be able to tell her how glad

I was she had come. I was also delighted to see Marn and Elani whirling by in each other's arms, joy on their faces. And I noticed that Nadir and Ramule were constantly in each other's company until they disappeared together into the night.

Much as I was glad to see others enjoying themselves, for myself I was less than happy. It wasn't only the situation with Adana that was causing me pain, but also my concern for Torvin and some feeling of responsibility for him. As the evening progressed I drank quite a bit of wine, too much in fact, something I rarely do, but it seemed to ease the pain and induce a sort of reckless forgetfulness if I just kept moving fast enough. Though the three women whose return we were celebrating left early along with their families, no doubt exhausted from the long journey and everything that had happened to them, I stayed almost to the end. I was reluctant to go to bed and try sleeping with all those churning thoughts and troublesome feelings to keep me company.

Groggy and out of sorts, I woke late the next morning to shouts and laughter and the unaccustomed sound of loud male voices. My head was aching, my mouth tasted sour and my stomach felt queasy. As I walked out of the house in my foul mood Ramule called out to me, "Look! You thought I was worthless, but you can see I'm really good for something after all. Nadir's been teaching me."

I looked up to see Ramule and Torvin on either side of our neighbor Garnith's house, replacing and fastening down a roof pole. Garnith herself was shouting encouragement to them and Nadir was standing below, calling out directions. At the sight of Nadir I felt all my anger come back. She had betrayed our whole settlement for Ramule's sake, trusting him not to run off even after everything I had told her about captives. What if he had left, gone to meet his father in secret before the exchange was made? Or even disappeared altogether? Then what would have happened? She had risked everything we had worked so hard for with her little game of love.

Looking at her, angry words stung my mouth. I started to say, "You could have..." but seeing the joy on Ramule's face and Torvin's as well, I swallowed my sharp words rather than spoil their day and their pleasure in useful work. After all, it was Ramule's first day of freedom and Torvin's first day of his new life.

Besides, it was over. What could have happened didn't. Ramule had honored his word. Our captured women had been returned. They were free, home safe with their loved ones. And we had even freed another woman. Dorial was here with us now, also busy in the yard, peeling poles. The other men had left and were being followed by Fedra and Rialin to be sure they headed back to the city. Only Ramule and Torvin remained, hard at work, lashing poles to the newly mended rafters of Garnith's house with Nadir laughing and shouting instructions and passing up peeled poles to them with the help of other women. It was another fine sunny day, and I was the only thing out of place there.

I gave them all a quick nod and said curtly, "Too much wine last night, bad head, need to work alone for a while." With that I walked away, taking the lash of my anger with me.

I gathered some tools from the big barn—a hammer and a metal bar—and went to a small shed at the edge of the common garden. It had been badly burned. The roof was gone and most of the boards were fire-damaged, but many of the upright poles were still usable and could be left in place for a new shed. I set to prying off the charred remnants of boards and tossing them in a pile, throwing my dark angry mood into my work. I was so noisy in fact that I didn't even hear Dorial until she was standing right next to me. By then I had worked up a good sweat, taken off my shirt and was in a much better frame of mind.

"Well, Solene, you certainly made yourself scarce. I've been looking everywhere for you. I wanted to thank you again for getting me out of that city. Last night I was too bewildered by everything new to be able to say much, but I'm very grateful to you. Of course you almost got me killed first. It was pretty close, but I guess I'll forgive you because you got me free instead.

"At first they couldn't wake Banya. You must have given her quite a dose. They had to throw cold water on her, then get her to her feet and walk her up and down. After that Peltron came with his men to haul us away. Torvin blocked his way in the hall, shouting that he had your letter in his hand and none of it was our fault. In fact he was waving the letter in Peltron's face. I don't think Peltron cared much if we were at fault or not. He was too angry. He wanted to hurt someone, and two serving girls looked like a handy enough target for his wrath. He certainly wouldn't have listened to our protests of innocence. If not for your letter he would have had us taken away, most likely to be tortured before being killed."

"I almost tore that letter up."

"Why would you do such a thing? Then we surely would have been blamed for your escape. Without that letter we would both be dead. I suppose you know about Banya. Torvin sent her home to her grandmother's to stay until the old woman gets better or dies. For a man he's not so bad, not bad at all really. I only wish they were all so kind, but then the world would be a very different place, wouldn't it? Did you ever think you might have killed Banya with such a big dose of that sleeping draught?"

"Dorial," I said with a laugh, "did you hunt me down to thank me or scold me or just pester me?"

"I came to thank you and also help you work."

"Didn't you hear me say I wanted to work alone?"

"I did and I came anyhow. I thought maybe enough time had gone by, but I can leave right now. Is that what you want?"

I sighed. "No, not really. I think I'd enjoy the company." I told her where to find some tools in the big barn. When she came back, we worked together for a while in concentrated, companionable silence since our tools made too much noise for easy conversation. I thought I might have to give her directions, but I saw right away that she had a practiced competence with tools and needed no instruction from me. I kept glancing at her, amazed to see her here with me in Nessian. When I was planning my escape she had been no part of the plans, except as an obstacle between me and my freedom, someone to be tricked and fooled.

When we took our rest, sitting side by side on a large rock, I turned to look at her, "Hard to believe, isn't it? Here we are, free women together for the first time. Not servant and master or prisoner and jailer, but free women belonging only to ourselves. Who knows, we might even get to be friends."

She grinned at me and shrugged. "Who knows, we might."

Later, job finished and in a much different mood, I walked home again. Ramule was sitting at a table in front of Garnith's house with Torvin and Nadir and several young women from our settlement. They were talking amiably as Garnith dished out big portions of stewed vegetables and grain. She gave me a nod. "If they're going to work so hard, they need lots of food to keep them going. Join us if you want, Solene." Ramule looked up at me as if trying to gauge my mood and know what sort of abuse to expect. I smiled, doing my best to look pleasant. "So, Ramule, you have made yourself our hostage all over again."

He blushed and laughed. Glancing fondly at Nadir, he said, "There are other ways of being held hostage. It doesn't always take a chain around your ankle. You can also be a hostage of the heart." Seeing his wide smile, I thought our sullen boy might actually be turning into a charming young man. I turned down the invitation, thinking he might be more comfortable without me at the table, but Dorial pulled herself up a bench and gave me a nod of parting.

The most painful thing that happened during that time was the funeral for the three old women who had died from the hardships of being forcibly moved, "our elders," as my mother called them reverently. Their bodies had been kept cool at the back of a cave and they were brought home for burial in one of the last wagons to leave the campsite in the hills. It was decided to bury them in The Grove, with some carved memory stones to commemorate the battle as well as the lives and deaths of these women since they were our fallen ones, the real casualties of that raid. Many were in tears around the newly dug graves, but Senli was the most distraught. She threw herself weeping on her great-grandmother's body. "Meme, why didn't you wait for me? I never got to say goodbye. Please speak to me. I need to hear your voice again. Why didn't you wait for me?" Finally her mother and aunts had to hold her back so the burial could take place.

After all their kin had spoken, Namuri climbed up on the back of the wagon to speak. Her voice quavered and there were tears in her eyes.

"Our beloved grandmothers had a right to die here at home among their loved ones and not be sent away into exile and discomfort in their final days. I think we need to set aside this day each year to honor their memory. We also need to mark and remember what happened here." She paused then and looked around at all of us. There was a long moment of silence before she spoke again. At last, with a expression of resolve on her face, she said, "I'm also taking this moment with all of you assembled in this place to say that I will be stepping down as Headwoman within the month. These events have taken too great a toll on me, and I fear I could not continue to serve you well. There are many others among you who could serve you better so there will be a choosing very soon."

Though I had been expecting this, it was still a shock. Namuri had been Headwoman for as long as I could remember. I wondered if Lucian would put her name in the choosing. She got things done efficiently enough, but she had none of Namuri's tact or kindness or patience, much-needed qualities in a Headwoman. Personally I would prefer Morith, though she was young to carry so much weight. I was quite surprised to see that it was Marn who came forward to help Namuri down from the wagon and get her up onto her horse and even more surprised to see how Namuri leaned into her and seemed to be talking to her in a friendly, easy manner.

In those first few days following Peltron's departure, a sort of peace settled over Nessian. Sometimes I would even hear voices raised in song or an instrument being played. It was not that things went back to normal. They would never be normal again, too much had happened, too much had changed and too many changes threatened in the future, but the frenzy with which we had been working eased. There was a little time now to swim in the river, or walk in the woods, or just sit and talk to a friend without feeling guilty for work not done. We even played some games of chance in the evening, scratching the lines in the dirt and tossing the pebbles.

Most of the roofs and sheds had been repaired and the gardens replanted where they had been trampled by horses. Except for Nadir, who would probably not leave until Ramule did, many of the friends and strangers who had come from elsewhere to help us had departed, emptying our big barn for our own use again. Our children and our old women—except for the three who died—were safely home. Our animals were back in their pastures and pens, and all our belongings back in place. Flowers covered Evandaru's altar and were constantly being replaced. The three young women who had been stolen away from us were home again and we had the pleasure of seeing them every day, walking free in our streets instead of having to fear for their lives, though I knew it would be a long time before they healed from their ordeal. And not to be forgotten, our hostage was a free man among us, no longer "an animal chained to a post" as Nadir had said. Best of all, we didn't have to be thinking of ways to kill him, as we had threatened to do if Peltron didn't make good on his promise. He was even helping to mend the damage his father had done.

And with all this was I full of joy? Not really. When I was a captive in Hernorium I vowed that if I ever got free I would thank the Goddess Evandaru every day and keep flowers on her altar; I would kiss our house post and the ground before the house each morning in gratitude. How quickly we forget. How easily we let small things turn into large ones.

One of the things that most irked me was the sight of Nadir, walking about our settlement as if she belonged, as if she had every right to be there, as if she had not betrayed us all by freeing Ramule that way. It surprised me that none of the other women seemed to be angry at her. Mostly I stayed clear of her when I could, but one morning, unavoidably passing her on the street, I couldn't resist saying, "You know, Nadir, if you stay with a man that way you will lose your right to live in the Women's Enclave."

She gave me a sharp, unfriendly look. "And why should you care? What business is it of yours, Solene?" Then she added with a shrug, "Besides, it doesn't matter. The Women's Enclave has grown too narrow for me anyhow. I need a wider world, one I can share with Ramule, the person I love." She was about to walk by, then turned back at the last moment and said with malice. "And who are you to talk? I saw the way you were dancing with Torvin. I notice how you disappear with him for long walks and talks. Why are you pointing your finger at me?"

Now I was really incensed. "Dancing is all you'll ever see, nothing more. Dancing vertically, not horizontally. Torvin and I are friends, only friends, that's all. And I never betrayed Nessian out of love for Torvin as you did with Ramule."

"Well, you see how it all turned out. I trusted him and I was right about him and you were wrong. I suppose that doesn't sit too well with you, does it?"

I flushed with anger and was about to make some clever, angry retort when I felt a hand on my arm. I turned to see my mother looking at me with concern in her eyes. She had likely heard most of this exchange. I was suddenly embarrassed. "I need to talk with you, Solene." Though she spoke very quietly, I knew from her tone that this was not a time to argue.

I gave Nadir a curt nod and followed Elani back to the porch of our house. She motioned for me to sit and sat down beside me. "It's not yours to judge, Daughter. You need to let it go and move on. Yes, she did a wrong thing, but it was a mistake she made for love and in the end nothing bad happened. Please, child, don't hold onto all that anger. I don't want to see you eaten up with bitterness like your grandmother." *Or your sister*, I heard in her unspoken words. "You need to heal your heart. You have to be able to weep for what happened to you." She put an arm around me and pulled me close. "Tears are more healing for the heart than anger."

Bristling, I started to say, "I don't need to cry, I need to..." when suddenly my breath caught in my throat, a huge sob came up almost choking me and the tears began to flow. With a groan I put my head down in her lap and wept like a child, cried as I had when I was little and hurt and the world seemed cruel and my mother was the only comfort in my life. She stroked my hair and murmured words of caring that I couldn't really understand but understood anyhow. Finally, as my sobbing stilled, I heard her say, "My poor baby, my dear sweet loving child, how I wish this had never happened to you—but it did. And now we have to find a way to heal the pain."

"It hurt so much. I was so afraid, I thought he would kill me. No one has ever hurt me that way before. I hate him! I wish him dead! It's hard not to hate his son. How can she love him that way?" I sat up slowly, shaking my head in a sort of daze of grief and confused feelings.

"The son is not the father. With a lot of courage, Ramule separated himself from all that. We should give him credit for it, not hate him. Besides, you love Torvin and he's the brother."

"But that's different."

"Not so different. You have to forgive or you'll make yourself sick."

"Not Peltron. I'll never forgive Peltron."

"If you want vengeance on Peltron you've already had it. He came after you and by doing so he lost his son and his brother and some of his men and horses and his battle and his pride. Now he has had to go home and explain it all to his father, who can't be very kind and forgiving, and to his wife, who must be furious with him for bringing their son to this place. Looks like vengeance to me, a good hard dose of it. Of course nothing can make up for what he did to you, but even killing him wouldn't do that, only time and love can heal that hurt."

"I missed you so much in that city. I was afraid I would never see you again. When I was trying to escape the Palace and hesitating in the doorway, too frightened to move, I heard your voice saying, 'I miss you, Solene. I want you home again.' It's your voice that saved me and brought me back." I looked up at her and saw she was crying too.

She shook her head. "No. It's your own courage and ingenuity that brought you safely home. I don't know how I could have lived if you'd been gone for good, snatched away into that other world."

"And here I am making you cry," I said ruefully. I looked at her. "Are you happy to have Marn back?"

"More than you can possibly imagine! All those years without her, it was as if I was missing an arm. But even Marn couldn't have made up for losing you, thinking you dead or worse."

Namuri had also heard some of my exchange with Nadir. She found me later. "Solene, I understand you've been through a terrible ordeal, but you can't carry it around, using it like a spear that way to stab other people. We need peace here and we need healing, not more wounding that needs to be healed in turn. Come to see me if you need to talk about what happened to you and you feel your mother and friends are too close to be able to hear it, but don't keep punishing others for it. Understood, Solene?"

Eyes cast down, I gave her a silent nod. Namuri was a gentle leader, but she could be very firm and her word carried great weight. I had been clearly reprimanded and needed to take it to heart.

The return of our women had reawakened all my memories of my own ordeal. I found myself going about with a tight fist of anger in my belly, but I certainly wasn't ready to go talk to Namuri, not yet anyhow, not now. And I didn't want to do what she accused me of, use that anger as a spear against others. Thinking it might be better that way, I tried again to work alone. Again I was sought out, this time by Valdru. She looked as if she hadn't slept that night and maybe the night before as well. There were dark circles under her eyes and her cheeks were hollow. The look on her face told me how much she needed to talk so I instantly gave up any attempt at work, set down my tools and sat on a rock by her to listen.

She was shaking her head and her voice sounded despairing. "I have to talk to someone who understands, Solene, someone who has shared the experience. I know my mother and sisters love me. They mean well, but they have no idea what it's like on this side of it. Every time I try to talk about what happened, they tell me, 'You're home now, Valdru, you're safe, you should forget all about it.' As if I can forget for one moment what happened! Then they try to distract me, to jolly me out of what they call 'your dark thoughts.' Do they really think I want to be haunted by it that way? I would talk to Tarsel, but her anger is so hot it's like putting my hand in the fire, and Senli is of no use to me, gone somewhere beyond words. I fear for her but I can't reach her. I can't help her and she certainly can't help me. So I came to look for you, but if it's an imposition, if it's too much I can go away and..."

"Not too much," I said quickly, taking her wrist in a tight grip to keep her there. I turned to look straight into her eyes. "How could it be too much? When have I ever not listened to you or you to me, Valdru? I probably need to talk just as much as you do. I think I've been working so hard these past few weeks, moving so fast all this time, just trying to outrun my own memories."

And so we talked back and forth, back and forth for hours, talked about everything that had happened since we had last been together. She looked different to me. There was a hardness in her face, an edge of grief and anger that had never been there before. I suppose I also seemed changed to her. I told her the story of my escape and answered her questions about the Palace and the city since she knew far less about Hernorium than I did. I even talked to her about the rape, something I had closed up in a hard knot of silence inside, thinking no one wanted to hear such ugly things or could even imagine them happening. Valdru nodded. "Tarsel also got raped and beaten for trying to escape.

141

Talking to the other weavers I gather that rape is a common way for such men to subdue women and terrify them into submission. I suppose you could say I was the lucky one, being a weaver and valuable that way. I didn't get the worst of it. Also I don't have Tarsel's fierce, impetuous nature. Seeing what happened to her, I didn't even think of trying to get away. You were very brave to escape like that."

"I would have died otherwise," I said tersely.

She made me tell her several times and in detail about the raid. When I talked about rolling the boulders down and how men and horses had gotten trapped and crushed beneath them she got a look of such gloating pleasure on her face that it frightened me. "Horses I can grieve for. They're the innocents in all this. Those men—I could see all of them dead in front of me and not turn a hair. Their screams of pain would have given me pleasure. I could joyfully have rolled those rocks myself. I could have cut their throats with a knife in my own hands and seen their lives bleed away in the dirt."

I turned to stare at her in shock. This was my gentle childhood playmate and now she sounded as ruthless as one of Peltron's men. "Were they all so terrible then?" I asked in a near whisper.

"Yes! And we were so innocent and it was so unexpected. It came out of the blue, literally, a beautiful blue day. We were returning from visiting Nadir in the settlement of Hamlin, the four of us laughing and talking, enjoying the ride together. We had just stopped because Huldra needed to relieve herself. Personally I would just have spilled my waters by the side of the road the way men do, but she went to hide behind a bush and her modesty saved her. I had just been saying to the others, 'I wish we could have talked Solene into coming with us, but she never goes anywhere. Maybe next time we should tie her up and carry her off.' Oh Goddess, what a thing to say! We had no idea. Next moment they were on us, howling and screaming, grabbing us off our horses and knocking us to the ground. Yes, with a knife in my hands I could kill each of them, three times over, and not shed a tear or even lose my breakfast over it.

"We were terrified and they were awful to us. They kept us bound and apart from each other, forbidden to speak from the moment we were captured, hitting us if we cried. They kept talking about this Peltron and how pleased he would be, what a good catch they had made for him. 'Think of that, they were just coming down the path and right into our hands.'

"I never went to the slave pits. Peltron was indeed very pleased with me. Because of my weaving skills he sold me to a Weavemaster for a very good price. Senli, because she's so pretty, he gave to a friend to be his Lanati and now she won't talk about what happened there. Tarsel got the worst of it. Tall and strong and not at all pretty in the way they like, she was sold into the slave pits to be picked for a work gang."

I was almost afraid to ask, afraid what the answer would be. "And coming back, were they still so awful? Was Torvin?"

"Mostly different men coming back. Some of them showed us a sort of rough kindness, but we knew they would do anything Peltron commanded, so what good is that kindness? But Torvin, no, he was different. From the moment he came to buy me back from the Weavemaster he was nothing but kindness. The master was not really a bad man, just practical. He fed us well and didn't beat us. We were too valuable for that, I suppose, but he kept us chained to the loom so we couldn't escape. Torvin was outraged. 'How can you do that? They're women, not animals.'

"'Can't have them running off. It's too expensive to keep replacing them.'

"'And what if there's a fire?'

"'There would never be a fire here. I'm much too careful.'

"'But what if there was? They'd all be trapped, burned to death.'

"The Weavemaster shrugged as he turned the key in the lock and freed me from the chain. 'What can I say? Life is chancy.'

"'I'm giving you an order to take those chains off, no argument,' Torvin told him sharply.

"As we left I turned back to see my fellow weavers grinning and the Weavemaster scowling at Torvin's back.

"'Where are you taking me?' I asked him fearfully. 'Am I to be a Lanati?'

"He shook his head vehemently. 'No, of course not. I'm freeing you. I'm taking you home.' He sounded very angry, but I knew his anger was for the master, not for me. He had already freed Senli. Tarsel was hard to trace, and he almost didn't find her. I think he got to her just in time. She told us later she was ready to die rather than go on being a slave, but she had vowed to take her crew boss with her, kill him before they got to her. She said she was just waiting for an opportunity. I have no doubt she would have done it.

"Torvin was very kind on the way back, making sure we were fed and comfortable and had everything we needed. Peltron, on the other hand, made sure we understood how much he hated us. I think he hated Dorial especially because she chose to leave the city and go live in the Women's Enclave. He made it clear that he only restrained himself from doing us harm for the sake of his son. Tarsel liked to taunt him. She could get him to roar with rage. Torvin had to restrain Peltron several times. Then he and I would have to make peace again, smooth things over. Torvin would always end up by reminding Peltron, 'Ramule's safety is at stake here. That's all that matters, Brother. You have to keep that in mind, no matter what.' Hard to believe that after all that Ramule refused to go home with him. Would you really have killed him if Peltron hadn't brought us back?"

I felt chilled and a shiver went up my back. Could we have done it? Should we? Would Namuri actually have ordered such a thing? Who would have carried out that order? I shook my head. "We'll never know now, will we? Thank the Goddess for that."

"Speaking of the Goddess, where was Evandaru when all this was happening? Did She abandon us? Has She gone elsewhere? Though I put flowers on her altar in gratitude for our safe return, I'm not sure She deserves them."

I might have been shocked by her words before my time in Hernorium. Now there was little that could shock me. I had also asked myself the same questions. We talked for a long while after

144

that and hugged and cried together and then talked again. I think it helped us both. I could feel that knot of rage and pain loosening a little, but the next time Valdru sought me out she seemed even more distraught. "I dream about them, almost every night, the other weavers. I see their faces. I hear their voices. They call to me, reaching out their hands, begging me to come back and free them. They say, 'Why you? Why not us?' What can I tell them? It's not fair. Why am I out when they're still trapped there?

"I'm home, I'm safe, I'm free and yet I'm not free, not really. And maybe I never will be. It was such a short time and it changed me forever, opened a door on a whole other world, one I knew nothing about. Now I can't seem to rid myself of it. When I thought I was there forever, that it was going to be my life, I began thinking of ways to kill myself."

I was nodding as she spoke, remembering my own fear and resolve. "I understand. When I made my escape I told myself I was either going to get free that day or die." At that Valdru started to cry. I wrapped my arms around her and held her close until she was calmer. For myself, I couldn't cry. It was as if I had worn out my tears.

Now that Torvin had made his declaration of being a Santeel, I was no longer uneasy in his presence. As he was clearly neither potential suitor nor potential master, I was able to see him more as a real person—not as the heir to Hernorium or the Magistrar's son or Peltron's brother—but simply as Torvin, a gentle, caring man. I think he was also seeing himself in a new way, exploring what this sudden freedom might mean for his life. He made friends with Sasha, Josian's dog, who ordinarily didn't like men, and she began following him around. He made friends with the other dogs in the settlement and they also followed him. He made friends with the children and took them down to the river to play. He even made friends with some of the women of the settlement, Marn, for instance, since she was not so shy of men, having passed as one herself for all those years. He learned how to plant crops and saw boards and hammer nails and even how to cook soup, and he seemed delighted with all these very ordinary things he had never done before in his privileged life. He enjoyed it all. Nothing seemed to be beneath him. There was a joy about him as if some huge weight had been lifted from his back and he was able to stand straight for the first time in his life. I came by one day when he and Ramule were working together, hoeing in the common garden. Torvin had a big grin on his face as he held up his hands to show me. They were tanned and scratched and there was dirt under the nails. "Look, Solene, blisters. Soon they will turn into calluses. Can you believe it?"

During that time we shared walks and long talks and I grew even fonder of him, yet I knew this couldn't last much longer, that he couldn't really stay. If I said anything like that to him he would nod thoughtfully and look sad. "I know I have to leave soon, but I prefer my life here to the one I had before. Soon I will have to decide where to go. Not back to the city of Hernorium, that much is clear. It wouldn't be safe. My declaration won't be forgotten by those men, not even on Peltron's orders. Too late anyhow. By now they're back and I'm probably the talk of the whole city." It amazed me how easily this stranger, who had been my enemy, had become part of my life and found his way into my heart.

More and more often now I found myself working next to Dorial—plastering and painting, trying to restore things to their former beauty—her choice, I believe, rather than mine, though I had no objections. I enjoyed her company, but sometimes I would find her looking at me strangely or even staring. I actually had the sense of her watching me as I went about my day. Finally I asked her if there was something the matter. She blushed deeply, looked awkward and embarrassed and then began stumbling over her words. "No, no, nothing's the matter. It's just that Josian tells me you and Adana are no longer together and so I wondered...well, I thought possibly...I meant to ask if you would consider...what I'm trying to say is might you think of teaching me something of the art of loving women since I seem not to do very well in that way with men?" She blurted out the last words all in a jumble.

The quaint way she said it made me laugh. Immediately she turned away, about to stalk off, hurt pride now added to embarrassment. I quickly grabbed her arm to hold her back. "Stop, Dorial, how can you make me such an offer and not wait for the answer? You haven't even given me a moment to think. I wasn't making fun of you. You just took me by surprise. In truth, I'm touched, no one has said anything so nice to me in a very long time." I took her hand and pulled her closer, looking her in the eye. "Is that why you've been watching me that way?"

She nodded. "I was trying to get up the courage to ask. Not an easy thing to do, so I've been waiting for the chance."

"What makes you think I would be a good teacher for you?"

"Because you're the one I want," she answered without a moment's hesitation.

Now it was my turn to blush. Then I shrugged. "Well, why not? I find you attractive; I enjoy your company. I think it had never occurred to me because I still can't seem to let go of my attachment to Adana, though, of course, we're separated by mutual agreement. My mind knows it's time to release her, long past time, but my heart keeps yearning after her, even though there's no way we can put a life together. I think I keep clinging to Adana because of our shared past, unwilling to admit that our past is not our future and hasn't been for a very long time. Maybe you can be *my* teacher too, help me find a way to close that door and open a new one."

"It would be my pleasure," she said softly as she drew me close, pulling me into her arms. She gave me a long, deep kiss and I wasn't at all sure who the teacher was going to be. We had to go back to our work, but we made a plan to meet that evening.

It felt strange to share with Dorial the bed I had shared with Adana for so long, but perhaps that was what was needed to break the spell. We lit one candle and I kept being surprised at seeing a stranger's face in place of the familiar one—but excited too. For her part, Dorial needed no teaching, only the slightest guidance. In truth, it was permission she needed, not instruction. I could feel her trembling with barely restrained longing and desire, hungry for something that was such a natural part of my life and had been so forbidden in hers. I was momentarily hesitant, afraid that Peltron's violation might block the way, but Dorial's touch and her intentions were so different that I found myself opening instead. When she trailed her hair back and forth across my breasts, any resistance melted away and all my own hunger and longing rose to meet hers.

I was falling under the spell of her kisses and caresses when suddenly a fierce anger came bubbling up through the loving, anger for everything that had happened to me. I found myself using my teeth and nails, fighting and struggling instead of surrendering. Dorial didn't seem to mind. She met me wherever I was. We tussled back and forth. Sometimes she pinned me down or imprisoned my wrists so I could throw all my strength against her strength, but she never held me so hard I felt trapped. Then the anger subsided as quickly as it had risen, and I was able to let myself sink into pleasure.

Afterward, as we lay gently stroking each other's bodies, I asked her about her experiences of loving. "Surely this wasn't your first time with a woman? You needed no teaching."

"Yes and no. I've been with girls when I was younger, just play between us really, and then later with women, but always a quick and fearful snatching of pleasure, afraid of discovery or betrayal, afraid that this time it might really cost me my life. This was my first time in freedom. A very different experience, I can tell you that."

I was amazed at how comfortable I felt with this stranger, how easy it had been. As I lay there next to her, floating in pleasure and thinking how different our lives had been, my mind suddenly drifted back to Hernorium. "I wish Banya had been able to come with you."

Abruptly Dorial pulled herself away. "I don't." Her answer was surprisingly sharp as she raised herself up on one elbow to look down at me, her expression suddenly hard. "This isn't the place for her. She wouldn't be happy here. She likes the noise and crowds of the city streets. This place would frighten her, too vast, too empty, too many trees and too few people. She likes working in the Palace. She thinks it a privilege, a big step up from living in the 'hovels.' She loves the bright lights, the fancy clothes, the gossip, the parties, the important happenings. She forgets she's just a servant there and feels as if she's really part of it all. For me, I feel it's the first time in years I can stretch out and really be myself." From this burst of words I understood that regardless of Banya's wishes in the matter, Dorial really didn't want her here, didn't want her dragging Hernorium and all that past with her into this new place that Dorial was trying so hard to make her own.

"Don't you miss the city at all?"

"I miss some of my friends there, but no, I don't miss the city, not with all the violence and cruelty I've seen there. I would much rather be here in this place with women, building houses and making a new life for myself. In Hernorium I was a servant, not exactly a slave but not free either. And I never forgot it, not for one moment. Here I'm a free woman with my future in my own hands. I'm more grateful than I can say that you made it possible for me to leave the city. And this," she gestured to me and then to the room, "this is better than anything I ever could have dreamt of or imagined. To be loving another woman and not be afraid for my life. What a gift, what a luxury. Are you willing to do this again or is this to be my only lesson?"

"Oh no, I think we have to try again. Surely there's more to be learned, though I'm not sure who's the teacher and who's the student."

"Maybe that's how it should be with lessons." With that she pulled me to her again.

We did indeed have more lessons, as many as we could find time for. In some strange way Dorial had given me back to myself, given me back my body that after the rape had become just a wooden thing for carrying my head about. She had freed me into my own life, helping me heal from both the rape and the loss of Adana. My life had taken a sudden turn. I went about singing.

There was joy in my heart again. I no longer felt as if I had a hidden wound that was slowly bleeding me away. My mother and Marn gladly accepted Dorial into our lives and what there was left of our house, but Karil said the space was too crowded for her and she moved into one of the tents with Adana.

After a few days of being with me, Dorial said, "If I'm going to live here among you I need to know more, especially about this contract or compact or agreement or whatever it is I keep hearing all of you talking about. How did this Women's Enclave come into existence and what has kept it safe all these years? I can't imagine how such a thing could come to pass."

I started to explain and then was embarrassed to realize how little I really knew. "Namuri would be a much better person to ask."

When we talked to Namuri, she nodded, saying many of the children had also been asking her questions. "My time is limited and so is my energy. I would much rather say it all just once. Come to the meeting circle tomorrow morning and I'll tell all of you that bloody old story again."

Actually her audience that next morning was a surprising mix of children and adults. "Look what you started," I said to Dorial as we struggled to find a place to sit. Evidently I wasn't the only one who had forgotten or never learned enough, or perhaps we were all just glad for a pause in the hard work. And after this raid, it suddenly seemed very important that we know our history better. I felt as if I was back at lessons again and should try hard to remember everything so I could recite it back perfectly and please my teacher. Looking from one to the other of the children's bright eager faces, I thought how close they had all come to losing their young lives.

The girls had formed their own little circle to one side, a sort of circle within the larger one so they could be together, wanting to be near the rest of us but finding security in each other after everything that had happened. Frightened and excited and needing to know how all this affected their lives, they kept touching each other, whispering and twittering together, but fell silent, all attention, the moment Namuri started to speak. Of course it's not as if we had never heard these stories before. It was just that they had never been so immediate and meaningful in our lives.

Namuri looked very grave, and her voice, when she began to speak, had the weight of ancient sorrows in it. "I have to warn all of you, this is a bloody story, not a pleasant one and not really suitable for children, so if any of you need to leave at any time feel free to do so.

"To start with, it wasn't always the way it is now. Back a few hundred years there were many wealthy cities in the West Country, some of which still exist today. Those cities were ruled by men who called themselves Magistrars or princes or kings, men who saw themselves as the supreme power there and thought the wealth of the cities belonged to them. As the cities grew they began intruding into each other's territory—or their assumed-to-be or claimed-to-be territory. What began as little border clashes with accusations of deceit, treachery and invasion soon escalated to actual battles with cities making shifting alliances in their struggle for power. There was little prospect for peace at the time. You might even have been considered a traitor if you talked of peace rather than absolute victory.

"All this had devastating results for country people caught between enemies. Their fields and villages were marched through and set on fire, and they were often slaughtered for being in the way of opposing armies. Finally the whole of the West Country was embroiled in an ongoing, unwinnable war that left an ever-widening path of devastation, with every city, town, village and settlement caught in that net of death. Those were terrible times. The Blooding, it was called, or The Killing Times. Those who didn't die of actual wounds often died of sickness or starvation.

"Women grew desperate. Unable to feed themselves or their children, they still kept getting pregnant and having babies. Men came home needing release from the horrors of battle and forced themselves on their women, or enemy men raped them as punishment or as the spoils of war. In despair and in

151

protest women began taking a pledge with each other and killing themselves and their children and especially their babies in the streets of the cities. Sometimes there were piles of women's and children's bodies in public places, but men were so blood-blinded they hardly seemed to notice. It didn't even slow them down. Then some women began gathering and planning to leave altogether. 'Why should we kill ourselves for them? Why not leave, go make a new life for ourselves somewhere else?' By then, men were losing control over their women because so many men were being sucked into the conflict.

"After making the beginnings of a life in the wilderness, some of the women came back to the cities, a delegation chosen and sent by the rest of them to shape a peace. Only women could come together across the bitter city divisions to save their children and the future. Men were too deeply embroiled in their quarrels with each other. They would rather die than make peace with their enemies. Finally women were able to force the peace because men were far too exhausted from the fighting. There was a saying current at that time, 'There will never be peace until women make that peace.' It had to happen. The way things were going then soon no one would have been left alive. All of West Country would have been food for buzzards and rats.

"Those women dictated the terms, telling the men that unless they stopped the fighting and agreed to the compact all the women would leave for good and life in the cities would end. There would be no women and therefore no more children and the cities they were fighting over would die. Part of the agreement was that there were to be no more armies and not any more men under arms than were needed to keep order in the streets. Also no rulers, no more of those men whose pride and greed had brought the whole region down in ruin. Cities that broke the agreement were to be isolated, no trade out and no trade in.

"Councils now run the cities instead of rulers, a big change from those days when women had no power and men killed everything that moved. Women sit on those councils and are as likely to be chosen Head-of-Council as men, though I have to tell you, that part was a struggle, hard to come by. For some men that was the worst of it, not the grief that their cities were in ruins, that everyone they knew was dead or even that they themselves might have lost their lives, but the much greater horror that women might rule over them. They thought it unnatural.

"After the fighting ended and the pact was signed, many of the women came back to rebuild the cities and take their rightful place there. But almost as many stayed in the wilderness, carving out a life there. And that was an important part of the contract, that women could create their own place to live, undisturbed by men and protected by West Country, part of it and yet set apart from it, protected and respected. Women were to be given whatever they needed to start this new life. And still it was hard with so much destroyed."

Dorial reached over, squeezed my hand and whispered in my ear, "A compact, an agreement that keeps women safe. I like that. It gives me hope."

I leaned toward her and whispered back, "But this time it didn't work. Peltron broke the compact."

Namuri went on, "It's almost two hundred and fifty years since the Killing Times. It took fifty years or more for West Country to begin to recover from its wars and another hundred and fifty for things to return to normal and then another fifty for the region to finally start prospering. During that time the Women's Enclave became well established, grew and flourished. We have lived in peace with men all these years. No way do we want to go through all that again. We don't think about it that much anymore, we just live here, but that is our history and our past." When Namuri stopped speaking there were tears in her eyes.

After a moment of silence one of the girls asked, "Why didn't all the women stay in the Enclave? Why did any of them go back?"

"I would have been one of those that stayed," I said quickly.

"I would have too," Dorial echoed.

"Yes, without a doubt," Namuri said, now smiling along with

her tears. "Both of you would have been like Solene's great-great-great-grandmothers. But many women felt they had a stake in the cities, that the cities belonged to them too, not just to those men. And also they had deep ties of affection—families and friends and neighbors they didn't want to abandon. Besides, it was hard shaping new places in a wilderness, desperately hard. Women had to adapt to a whole new way of living, acquire many new skills, things they had been forbidden to learn. Some of them starved to death, some of them froze. There were hard winters, wild animals, not an easy life. We need to be grateful to those who carved out the ease and pleasantness with which we now live."

Now Karil spoke up. "I almost envy them, being there at the very beginning, seeing it start, shaping the future."

"Don't envy them. It was a terrible, harsh time with many deaths. Just be thankful for what they built for us."

Then Marn stood up. "Didn't the people of Hernorium sign the agreements along with everyone else?"

"Yes, of course, but they were just a village then or maybe a small town. They've grown into a city, and it seems as if they've forgotten lessons learned. There's been talk lately of Hernorium much exceeding the pact in the number of men under arms, yet we did nothing. There has been peace for so long I suppose none of us wanted to envision the possibility of war again."

Josian asked, "Does this mean we are going to have to warn the West Country to raise armies for defense, when that goes against the compact?"

Namuri nodded, "Something must be done to enforce the compact or enforce the sanctions, but unfortunately it's never long before troops assembled for defense get restless and begin to fight their own little wars of aggression. At first they say it's to make themselves safer or to practice and keep in shape. Soon it's for the pleasure of conquest, because it's fun, because they can do it, because they grow stale with all that peace and nothing real to do. They come to liberate and stay to oppress. And those who are being freed are never quite grateful enough or generous enough or show gratitude in the right way."

Hearing Namuri tell those old stories again, I felt a chill run up my back. Things were shifting, new patterns emerging, and we were all part of those new patterns, bound together in them. Myself and Dorial and Namuri and Torvin and Ramule and Marn and even Peltron, even the Magistrar in his faraway Palace. Things the end of which we could not even imagine had already been set in motion.

In the end it was Dorial rather than Adana that I took to my enchanted secret place in the woods. Not even Torvin had been there, in spite of his dream. One afternoon she and I were hard at work together, hammering and sawing on some new shelves for Elani's kitchen when Marn sought us out. We were making so much noise she had to clap her hands loudly before we even noticed she was there. "You've both worked too hard for too long. Why don't you stop for a while, take the afternoon off, go do something you both enjoy, a walk through the orchard, a swim in the river, anything, and leave us a little peace and silence in this house. I can finish these later." I was about to argue. Dorial gave me a sharp look and I quickly put down my hammer.

It was deeply satisfying to take her there, to share it with her. As thrilled with the beauty of the place as I had been, she threw her arms wide and turned in all directions. "Perfect, just perfect, so beautiful, like a dream."

I told her then about Torvin's dream. She gave me a long thoughtful look. "Strange, as if his dream was beckoning him out of his old life and into his future. But this is not a place to bring a man, this is a place for us." Then she reached out to stroke my hair. "In Hernorium I was always looking for any excuse to touch your hair. It made my fingers itch with desire, wanting to dress and arrange it, even though Banya was much better at such things than I was. In fact, I was always trying to find an excuse to touch any part of you."

"And now you can touch as much of me you want to." I reached out to take off her shirt.

She let me do it, but then she shook her head, looking worried. "I've never done this outside. No one will see us here?"

"No one would care, but in truth no one comes here. This is my own secret place. No one but Evandaru will see us."

"Then let's make pleasure for her eyes," she said with a grin as she reached for my shirt.

After that we stripped off the rest of our clothes, scattering them about carelessly as we sank down together into the soft moss. This time there was none of that hunger, desperation and anger that had marked our first time together. No longer strangers to each other in that way, we both moved languidly and sensually as if under the spell of this place. Pushing me down, Dorial ran slow damp kisses along my whole body until I was shivering all over with pleasure and desire. Just before release I rolled her over and did the same to her. Then we used hands as well as mouths until we both cried out together, free to make all the noise we wanted with only the birds to hear.

Afterward, laughing and shouting, we rolled together down the mossy bank and into the pond. Though it looked dark and somewhat forbidding, it was warmer than one might have expected. The water felt silky on the skin and the sand was soft underfoot. We rubbed our wet bodies against each other, nipping and nuzzling like two water creatures.

Later, as we lay drying on the moss in a patch of sunlight, I propped myself up on my elbow to look at her naked body. So lovely, lush skin again the green velvet of the moss, dark hair spread out in waves. Seeing me watching her she said suddenly, "Adana was a fool to give all this up."

Instantly I found myself bristling in Adana's defense. "Adana was never here," I said sharply.

"I don't just mean this place. I mean you and this place and everything here. I would never trade this for the city, any city, no matter how grand. No room in the Palace can equal this."

"Adana has business elsewhere," I said in that same sharp tone.

She gave me a knowing grin. "No need to be defending her,

even if she is a fool."

Suddenly I relaxed. She was right, no reason to be defending Adana. She didn't need it. I had brought the right person here, someone who could love this place as much as I did. If I had brought Adana, I would have been watching her face eagerly, hoping for signs of pleasure, hoping she could see how beautiful it really was. And she would have been impatient, eager to be away. To her it would have been just one more place in the forest where she didn't want to be anyhow, nothing special. I would have been trying to use it as a way of luring her into staying and she would have been resisting, setting her will against mine. Of course I would have been hurt again. We probably would have had one more fight and the magic of this place would have been spoiled for me.

Dorial was watching my face as I worked all this out for myself. Finally I grinned back at her and said in a much softer voice, "Adana has business elsewhere. You and I have business here." Then I rolled over, covering her body with mine, pressing my lips to hers and my legs between her legs. It was almost dark before we got back. The shelves were neatly finished. They already had some goods stacked on them. Elani and Marn were even beginning to worry about us.

As the days went by I grew more and more accustomed to Torvin's presence among us. I knew I would miss him when he left. We had never been lovers, of that I was glad, but we were something more than friends, a thing I couldn't even name. It was almost as if he was my sister, if a sister could be kind and loving instead of hateful and jealous, or perhaps the brother I would never have. Then, one morning, as I was going to the well to get water for our house, Namuri stopped me and drew me aside. "He can't stay here forever, you know," she told me with some annoyance. "You're the one who knows him best. You have to be the one to tell him that it's time to leave."

I had no question who she meant. "But he doesn't know where to go," I protested.

"Not our problem. We can't have men taking up residence in Nessian because they don't know where else to go. This is much longer than any man has ever stayed here."

"And what about Ramule?"

"Ramule and Nadir are planning to leave very soon. And besides, Ramule is not your problem. I think that Torvin is. You have this unnatural affection for him."

I bristled at those words, wanting to argue that my affection for him was not unnatural, but I kept my silence and nodded. Namuri was right, I was the one who had to tell him.

I supposed Torvin was down at the river with the children. I heard shouts and bursts of laughter coming from that direction. I dreaded doing this. Yes, I should be the one to say it but I didn't want him to leave, and now I would be the one to send him away. Who knew if I would ever see him again? I was afraid for him in that hostile world out there. At least here he was safe.

As I started to walk down to the river I heard Namuri calling the children. They came up, dashing past me, helter-skelter, still laughing and shouting and almost running into me in their rush. Torvin came walking up more slowly. It grieved me to see how his face changed from a look of joy and pleasure to a look of sadness and worry when he saw me. He must have read the expression on my face.

"Namuri asked me to speak to you. She says it's time for you to go," I blurted out.

"She's right. It's time and long past time. I know I've overstayed my welcome and my usefulness here, but truthfully I don't know where to go. What do you suggest, Solene?"

"Me? I'm not the one to ask. Except for that brief forced time in Hernorium, this place is all I know of the world. We should go ask Josian and do it now; I think she's planning to leave soon. She's been everywhere and knows everything. Surely she can tell us something."

When we found Josian she was repacking her entire wagon in preparation for departure. She had taken everything out and laid it all on the old piece of oiled canvas she used to cover her wagon when the rains came. All her belongings and her wares were stacked here and there in colorful chaotic disarray and she was inside, singing and sweeping. When I called to her she came out, sat on the tailgate of the wagon and said somewhat impatiently, "Is this a social visit, Solene, or do you need something from me? If it's a visit I have no time now to chat. I'm trying to leave. How on earth did I manage to trap myself in one place for so long? I never stay anywhere more than a few days. Your women at Nessian must have cast a spell over me." I had heard stories of Josian among our women and thought the spell might well have been cast from the other direction.

I gave Torvin a nod. "Tell her what you need."

When he stood there, silent and indecisive, I gently pushed him forward. "Tell her what you need," I prompted again.

After another moment of wordless hesitation he finally blurted out, "I can't go back to Hernorium. What's said can't be unsaid again. It would mean my death to return. But I don't know where else to go that would be better, and I can't stay here any longer."

Josian cocked her head and looked at us thoughtfully. "A problem, yes, but nothing that can't be solved. You came to the right person. I know of a city where men like you live openly and no one bothers them."

"Many men?"

"Enough."

"And truly no one bothers them?"

"No one cares. They are simply part of the life of the city."

"Would they help me?"

"Yes, of course. They would be glad to take you in. That's what they do. They would find you a place to live, some work you can do, companionship, whatever you need or wish."

"Can you tell me how to get there?"

She was silent for a while, staring into space and thinking while we waited anxiously, tense and silent, shifting from foot to foot. Then she nodded. "Better yet, I can take you there. Yes. Why not? I need to go to a city and get my trade moving again. I've

159

been off the road far too long already. Adana and Karil want to go to a city 'Outside,' out in the larger world, not in the Women's Enclave. It might as well be the city of Anthrim."

Torvin's look of mingled relief and gratitude made me want to weep. Josian was nodding again. She went on almost as if speaking to herself, as if she had forgotten we were even there. "Well, I've really burned the cake this time, haven't I? Beyond fixing, I'd say. I won't be going back to Hernorium any time soon myself. My friends will just have to do without my amusing stories. As soon as Peltron got back to the city after his little defeat here, I'm sure he had the Magistrar declare me a traitor for my part in all this, a traitor and fair game for any man's weapon. All the guards of the city will have been told to watch for me with their swords ready."

"You did that for us? Gave up your trade with Hernorium and put yourself in danger for our sake?"

She shrugged and shook herself as if shaking off a spell. "No, not just for you here in this settlement. I did it for all of us here in the West Country. If they start raiding for women in this region, then the compact will be broken and useless, and none of us will be safe on these roads, certainly not me in my little wagon with only Sasha for protection. Besides, I enjoyed the challenge of winning against trained armed men who far outnumbered our swordswomen. A worthy game, well played, I'd say."

"Where will you go after Anthrim? Will you ever come back this way?"

A look of real sadness crossed her face. "Maybe I'll even stay there for a while, find a place for my wagon, get to really know some people. I have friends here, friends there, friends everywhere, but in truth no real friends. If I didn't come back on my trade route people would say, 'I wonder whatever happened to Josian,' but no one would really mourn me, not even my mother. She already thinks I live a dangerous life and expects me to die a violent death on the road. Only Sasha would care. Sasha and my horse Dapple are my only true friends, my real family. Yes, maybe it's time to settle for a bit, though of course I have to go around and warn people in the West Country about possible trouble from Hernorium." Then her expression changed again and she waved us away. "That's enough talk now. I already said I had no time to visit. On your way. You have what you want. Let me get back to work. Torvin, be ready to leave at any moment. Three more days, four at the very most."

After that everything was a bustle of departure with food, bedding and clothing being gathered, sorted and packed, in the wagon or in saddlebags. Karil, of course, was gathering her own things, trying to decide what to take and what to leave. She kept saying, "Who knows when I'll be back, if ever, I may need that, or that, or that." Not very kind to our mother who had a pained look on her face the whole time. I felt some guilt since I was the one who had set my sister's departure in motion. One morning I woke to the sound of my mother's weeping and came into the kitchen to see her in Marn's arms. Over her sobs Elani kept saying, "I almost lost one daughter and now I'm going to lose another. It's too hard. What have I done to bring such a fate down on my head?" Marn was trying to comfort her, but I knew that nothing Marn said or I said would really ease the pain.

Then, as the time grew short, advice was given, farewells were said, promises of letters were made, tears were being shed. When I heard Ramule complaining to Nadir, saying, "What am I to do? My father went off and didn't even think to leave me a horse," I quickly went down to the common pasture to look for Mercy. Being much too busy working in the settlement, I hadn't ridden her since coming home. And besides I had my own horse. She seemed to remember me and trotted over to rub her head against my arm. The shoe polish had all worn off and the white star between her eyes looked very bright against her dark face. I fed her a piece of apple, gave her a minute or so to chew it, then slipped on her bridle and rode without a saddle up to where Ramule was still talking with Nadir.

I saw his eyes go wide with surprise. "She looks just like my mother's horse, Brightstar."

"She is, only I called her Mercy because she carried me out

of captivity and brought me home again. I just borrowed her for a little while. She was the easiest one to take. I saw that she was already saddled and bridled, and no one was around at that moment to stop me."

I found myself protecting Monice even now. Who knew how things would turn out or what her son would become in the future. I was grateful to her for help no matter what her reasons, though I wondered how she was feeling now that she had lost her son and her husband had come home in disgrace. Did she hate me? Did she believe I was at fault? Did she ever think of me living in this distant place?

I slid off the horse in front of Ramule and handed him the reins. "You can have her now if you want."

He stared at me for a long moment, mouth open in surprise. Then he took the reins and put his arms around the horse's neck. "Of course I want her. I love this horse. And anyhow the one I rode here is gone. But why? I thought you hated me."

"I suppose I did, but I'm getting weary of hating. It's heavy; it weighs you down. Besides, it's not you I hate. It's what happened to me and hating you won't cure it. Anyway I think it's better for both of us if there's peace between us when we part."

Ramule nodded solemnly, looking quite serious for a moment. Then his expression shifted abruptly. With a whoop of joy he jumped on the horse's back and, shouting excitedly, galloped over to where Torvin was talking to Marn. "It's Brightstar! I have her back!" They both looked up startled as he galloped back again to Nadir, very much the boy at that moment, not at all the man he was trying so hard to become. When he slid off the horse's back into Nadir's open arms, I walked away quickly, not looking back because I could feel myself starting to cry and I very much didn't want to cry in front of them.

Elani and Marn had arranged a farewell gathering at our house for Karil and also for Adana, who had been like an extra daughter in our home for so long. Actually it was more Marn who arranged it, trying perhaps to reassert her presence in our house and in the settlement as well. Elani was too heartbroken about Karil's departure to be able to do much arranging, but she held her grief in check for the evening, no tears and no reproaches. She smiled graciously at our guests, served food all around and talked to everyone with her head held high and her eyes bright. Dorial, of course, was already there. In addition we had invited Nadir and Ramule and Torvin since they would all be traveling with Adana and Karil, as well as Valdru and her mother Lucian and her sisters, Garnith and her daughter Shandi and our neighbors on the other side. We would be honoring Josian who had helped us all so much, and of course Namuri would be there. It was quite a little gathering, the first such thing to happen in our house since the raid.

For that day and the whole day before we had been making preparations. Waxing all the wood, polishing the windows, scrubbing the floor and putting back those scraps of rug that had escaped the fire and were still intact, filling bowls with flowers and hiding the last of the damage, trying to make the house look as if it had never been destroyed. Just before people started to arrive I looked around our little home one more time and felt a thrill of pride, taking in the sight of our beloved possessions back in their places, the bright flowers in their pretty bowls and all the shining surfaces reflecting back at me. *Better than any palace,* I told myself with a grin.

Seeing our house fill with people that evening, I found myself torn between joy and grief. So much had happened. So much lost. So many new beginnings. My heart had hardened from what had happened to me. Now I had to let it open again if I was to have any hope of a loving future and not, as my mother kept warning me, "turn bitter like your grandmother." Evandaru forbid, not that!

For a while now I had felt myself softening toward Karil, becoming more accepting, even more loving. Deceiving myself that she was feeling the same way I sat down by her on the bench, choosing a time when no one else was nearby and I could have a moment alone with her. "I think you're very brave, Karil, going off to the city this way. I just wanted to tell you that I wish you well on this new venture of yours."

At those words she turned such a look of such venom on me that I wanted to jump back. "Do you really?" she said with a knife in her voice. "You wish me well? I think you actually wish me well gone, that's what I think. I'm sure it pleases you to have me away from here. Then you can have Elani and Marn all to yourself, or rather you can share them with that hard-faced outsider you've brought into this house in my place. I wish you had stayed in Hernorium. Things were better for me here with you gone, but Elani was breaking her heart over you. It grew tiresome listening to her weep."

I stood up. My face burned. I felt as if I'd been slapped. I wished Adana had been there to hear that exchange, though, of course, Karil would never have spoken that way in her presence. I was furious. I wanted to shout back in anger, but I knew it would only make matters worse, especially for our mother. Instead I held my temper and said quietly, "Don't you know how much it hurts Elani when you talk this way? She loves you very much, Karil, and only wants your happiness."

"Ah yes, Elani, she'll be glad too to have me gone. Then there'll be peace in her house and she and Marn can really do their little dance together. She doesn't need me here for that." There was a sly sexual inference in her words.

I felt myself bristle with anger and was about to walk away before I said anything that would blow our quarrel out in front of everyone and so spoil the evening, especially for Marn and Elani. Then, all in an instant, my feelings changed, going quickly from anger to disgust to utter weariness. In the next moment I was caught in a wave of pity so sharp it was like a physical blow to my heart. I almost gasped from the pain of it. Poor Karil! After all that had happened, after almost losing our homes and our lives and even our whole settlement, everything—there she was still caught in her old grievances as if nothing had changed.

Of course I could say nothing of that. Pity spoken would only have made matters worse between us. Yes, it was true, she needed to go away and start over and be shed of the past. I leaned over and spoke softly in her ear, "I hope you find what you need in this new place, Karil." I said it kindly. I meant every word from my heart, but I turned quickly to walk away before she could make an angry retort and re-engage my own anger. I was very tired of all this quarreling and wanted an end to it. For the rest of the evening I made sure to stay as far away as possible from Karil and her sharp tongue.

Going about, talking to the others, I managed to have a fine time at the gathering in spite of my sister. Later there was even some dancing in our yard with Valdru playing the flute and Garnith playing the five-stringed ashti. I danced with everyone in a sort of manic gaiety, even Ramule and Nadir, first separately and then together, and then with Torvin, saying goodbye in my heart. "No matter what a fine time you're having in your new life, you should keep an eye on your nephew," I told him. "He's very young for such a big adventure."

"Of course I will, of course, never fear," Torvin assured me as we whirled around to the music. I had already told Ramule, "Keep an eye on your uncle in that city, watch out for him. He's like an open door right now, an innocent. He may need your protection."

Then Garnith snatched Torvin away and suddenly I was dancing with Adana. "Sleep with me tonight, Solene, not as lovers but as old friends. I need to hold you close one more time."

I nodded. How could I refuse such an offer? "I have to tell Dorial." Instantly I went to find her. Not a problem, she told me, as she had already planned to go home with Valdru and her family. I was relieved and at the same time a little hurt by how easily she had passed me off. Perhaps, in her thoughtful way, she had anticipated Adana. Then, abruptly, the evening was over and people were begining to leave. Namuri went first, saying she was getting too old for such festivities. I actually hugged Ramule and Nadir and wished them well. When Torvin was leaving I wished him a good life in Anthrim and then surprised myself by kissing him on the mouth and found myself being kissed in return. It was hard to let him go. Josian and I hugged a long time before she left. "I still think I owe you my life," I told her. "And you certainly put yourself at risk to save Nessian. We are all greatly in your debt. I hope you come through again. If there's ever anything..."

She put one hand over my mouth and pinched me hard on the rear with her other one. "Enough of all that sentimental glop, Solene. I had a good time here and now it's time to move on. If I ever want anything from you I'll remember to just ask for it." With that she kissed me on the mouth much harder and longer than I had kissed Torvin and then whirled off into the night, the last of our guests to depart.

It wasn't until everyone had left, until after I had danced with Nadir and Ramule together and felt the humming energy between them, that I thought how grateful I should be to Nadir, how grateful we should all be to her for the great favor she had done us, not intentionally but from love, from her own heart. She had won over the Magistrar's grandson, Peltron's son, the boy rapidly turning into a man, who might well become the future Magistrar of Hernorium and so hold the fate of that city in his hands and our own fate as well. No matter what happened in the future, he would be a very different man than if he had never come here and never met Nadir.

Would Nadir become his wife? He had clearly said he would choose his own. I tried to imagine her in Monice's place. She would not be the timid and fearful wife, chosen without consent and afraid to speak her mind. She would be a woman of power in that city, the hand behind the throne or perhaps on the throne. I had to laugh, trying to picture her in Monice's fancy and restrictive clothes. No, she would not be one to wear skirts so tight at the ankle as to hobble her. She would stride about that city and set new fashions. But who knew what would happen in the future, what Peltron would really do. Would he actually disown his son? Mount an even bigger raid against us out of angered pride? As Josian had said, this was either the last battle of a very old war or the first battle of a new one.

Adana and I spent that last night together, not as lovers, just holding each other tenderly and saying goodbye. I kept thinking back to the time when I first escaped from Hernorium and Adana thought we could put it all back together. That was over now, no more such illusions.

"Dorial doesn't mind our being together?" she asked as she wrapped her arms around me and held me close.

I shook my head. "When I asked she said, 'Why should I mind? You've given me so much pleasure in such a short time, more than in my whole life. How could I you deny anything?' Besides, she had already planned to go off with Valdru's family."

I didn't ask if Karil minded. I suppose I didn't really want to know.

"Are you happy with her?" Adana went on.

"Yes, very happy."

"I'm glad. Are you still angry with me?"

"Not any more. How can I be? You need to go, I need to stay. It's that simple. What else could we do? I'll always care for you, Adana, but it's different now. Do you really love my sister Karil, or is she just someone for you to travel with?" She must have heard the skepticism in my voice.

"Yes, I really love her, but the person I love is not the person you know. She's different around you, less herself, more hostile, pulled off center by the force of your presence. It will be good for her to be gone from here, someplace new where she can be her real self, away from you and your mother and even from this settlement where everyone thinks they know her."

"Do you say the same to her about me?"

"Just the same. I tell her you're different around her, that she doesn't really know the person I love. I don't think she believes me."

"Well, I for one will be glad enough to be away from her. Every time I see her she's either glowering at me or gloating. It doesn't make for fondness."

"You see, time to be apart."

Trying to picture Adana in a city, I suddenly saw her in my mind's eye the way she had been the day of the raid, so fierce

167

and full of power. "I'll never forget the sight of you on top of Hawk Mound, shouting like a wild thing with flames coming up all around you and in back of you and even out of your hair. You terrified those soldiers. You were glorious, magnificent, unforgettable."

She slipped her hand over my mouth. "Hush, best not to think of me that way. That's a part of myself I hope never to meet again." I thought she might well need that part to keep herself safe in the city, but I kept my silence on it.

After that we talked of our shared past and our memories until it was almost dawn. Then came the sudden rush and bustle of final departure. Later I stood in the doorway of my mother's house with Dorial beside me, watching Josian's wagon drive away with Adana and my sister Karil and Torvin sitting on the seat beside her, their horses tied on behind. Torvin had Sasha in his lap and a look of melting contentment on his face. Nadir and Ramule were riding alongside, with Ramule looking very fine mounted on his mother's horse, Brightstar. I was glad I had returned her to him.

I raised my hand to wave to them and heard the little wagon bells start up as if in answer. Most of the settlement was there to see them off. I had regrets, many of them, and at the same time I had no regrets at all. Everything was as it should be. Now that my mother's house was fully mended, Dorial and I would begin building our own nearby.

**Publications from
Bella Books, Inc.**
The best in contemporary lesbian fiction

**P.O. Box 10543, Tallahassee, FL 32302
Phone: 800-729-4992
www.bellabooks.com**

ROOT OF PASSION by Ann Roberts. Grace Owens knows a fake when she sees it, and the potion her best friend promises will fix her love life is a fake. But what if she wishes it weren't? $14.95

KEILE'S CHANCE by Dillon Watson. A routine day in the park turns into the chance of a lifetime, if Keile Griffen can find the courage to risk it all for a pair of big brown eyes. $14.95

SEA LEGS by KG MacGregor. Kelly is happy to help Natalie make Didi jealous, sure, it's all pretend. Maybe. Even the captain doesn't know where this comic cruise will end. $14.95

TOASTED by Josie Gordon. Mayhem erupts when a culinary road show stops in tiny Middelburg, and for some reason everyone thinks Lonnie Squires ought to fix it. Follow-up to Lammy mystery winner *Whacked*. $14.95

NO RULES OF ENGAGEMENT by Tracey Richardson. A war zone attraction is of no use to Major Logan Sharp. She can't wait for Jillian Knight to go back to the other side of the world. $14.95

A SMALL SACRIFICE by Ellen Hart. A harmless reunion of friends is anything but, and Cordelia Thorn calls friend Jane Lawless with a desperate plea for help. Lammy winner for Best Mystery. Number 5 in this award-winning series. $14.95

FAINT PRAISE by Ellen Hart. When a famous TV personality leaps to his death, Jane Lawless agrees to help a friend with inquiries, drawing the attention of a ruthless killer. Number 6 in this award-winning series. $14.95

STEPPING STONE by Karin Kallmaker. Selena Ryan's heart was shredded by an actress, and she swears she will never, ever be involved with one again. $14.95

THE SCORPION by Gerri Hill. Cold cases are what make reporter Marty Edwards tick. When her latest proves to be far from cold, she still doesn't want Detective Kristen Bailey babysitting her, not even when she has to run for her life. $14.95

YOURS FOR THE ASKING by Kenna White. Lauren Roberts is tired of being the steady, reliable one. When Gaylin Hart blows into her life, she decides to act, only to find once again that her younger sister wants the same woman. $14.95

SONGS WITHOUT WORDS by Robbi McCoy. Harper Sheridan's runaway niece turns up in the one place least expected and Harper confronts the woman from the summer that has shaped her entire life since. $14.95

PHOTOGRAPHS OF CLAUDIA by KG MacGregor. To photographer Leo Westcott models are light and shadow realized on film. Until Claudia. $14.95

MILES TO GO by Amy Dawson Robertson. Rennie Vogel has finally earned a spot at CT3. All too soon she finds herself abandoned behind enemy lines, miles from safety and forced to do the one thing she never has before: trust another woman. $14.95

TWO WEEKS IN AUGUST by Nat Burns. Her return to Chincoteague Island is a delight to Nina Christie until she gets her dose of Hazy Duncan's renown ill-humor. She's not going to let it bother her, though. $14.95